THE WESSEX PAPERS

Volume 2

FALLOUT

Daniel Parker

AVON BOOKS
An Imprint of HarperCollinsPublishers

Fallout

For information address
HarperCollins Children's Books, a division of
HarperCollins Publishers, 1350 Avenue of the Americas, New York,
NY 10019.

 Produced by 17th Street Productions,
an Alloy, Inc. company
151 West 26th Street, New York, NY 10001

Library of Congress Catalog Card Number: 2001118924
ISBN 0-06-440807-8

First Avon edition, 2002

AVON TRADEMARK REG. U.S. PAT. OFF.
AND IN OTHER COUNTRIES,
MARCA REGISTRADA, HECHO EN U.S.A.

Visit us on the World Wide Web!
www.harperteen.com

First, Some Important
Documents to Review . . .

Excerpts from Sunday Winthrop's contribution to the Wessex Academy's "time capsule": a sealed tube full of anonymous personal essays that is buried at the beginning of every senior year, then unearthed twenty-five years later as an ongoing study of sociological trends at boarding school.

"Membership has its privileges."—American Express.

That's going to be my senior quote. I figure if I tell you children of the future my senior quote, then you'll be able to figure out who wrote this little essay. (And if my daughter's among you, hi, honey!) That way I won't be anonymous. After all, what's the point of doing something if you can't take credit for it?

*   *   *

. . . Teen angst? Forget about it. I'm part of a select group, the children of the most powerful alums—the elite. "ABs" we're called. "Alumni Brats." We rule the school. Everybody knows it. There's no point in trying to act polite or pretending we're just like everyone else. Membership *does* have its privileges. . . .

        Carter Boyce
        Hadley Bryant
        M. Hobson Crowe III
        Chase Edward
** <u>Noah Percy</u>
        Allison Scott
        Boyce Sutton IV
        Spencer Todd
        Mackenzie Wilde
        Sunday Winthrop

** Don't bother going through the time
capsule submissions. We should go with NP.
That slacker ennui is an act. So are the
lame jokes. He <u>loves</u> W. Even more than the
others, I'd say. Just like his father.
Definitely the best candidate so far. Also,
we should keep an eye on FW. He's a wild
card.

- - - - - - - - - - - - - - - - - -

Agreed. I'll make the necessary
arrangements. The PBs are confirmed for
Phase One. We'll set this year's asking
price at $200K. And don't worry about FW.
He'll fall into line soon enough.

Dear Noah,

I just wanted to apologize for my inappropriate behavior the night of the Student Council Dinner. I must have had too much wine. I'd like to talk to you, if you have the chance. I'll be at home all evening. I'm the dorm advisor in Meade Hall, in case you don't know.

Sincerely,
Miss Burke

A Segment of Noah Percy's Wesleyan Application

Part 3: *In two hundred words or less, describe an incident you regret and the lesson you learned from it.*

I Know That Sleeping With a Teacher Was Wrong, But She's Hot

It's the old boarding-school daydream, the subject of countless films and pulp novels. A male student fantasizes about being seduced by a young, sexy, female teacher . . . and it comes true.

But what if it were to happen in real life?

Well, it happened to me last night. And I'm still trying to figure it out. It certainly has nothing to do with my appearance. I enclose a picture as evidence. . . .

The Manifesto of SAFU (pronounced *sah-FU*): Sunday and Fred United

We, the undersigned, do solemnly swear:

1) Never to use any abbreviations (SAFU excepted) when talking to each other.

2) To devote ourselves fully to making people at Wessex see the absurdity of their own lives (ours included).

3) To unite the student body against hypocrisy and cliquedom.

4) To find out, once and for all, why an oaf like Paul Burwell can be allowed to keep a job as a math teacher at Wessex for twenty years.

5) To find out why Paul Burwell (or whoever else it could have been) planted chewing tobacco on Tony Viverito.

6) To get Kate Ramsey put on the student council.

7) To get Allison back (in a very fitting way, as yet to be determined) for making the first few weeks of Sunday's senior year hell.

8) To sabotage any and all Alumni Brat events.

9) To kill Sven Larsen.

10) Okay, maybe not #9. **But everything else.**

Sunday Winthrop

Frederick Wright

Part I
"Baby, Let's Get Freaky!"

Sunday Winthrop knew she was in serious, serious trouble. It was almost funny, in a way—funny in the sense of being horrifying and not funny at all.

It wasn't just that she was committing four major offenses simultaneously. True, she had entered a boy's room without permission (a coed visitation violation: Sunday detention). And yes, it was past two in the morning (a curfew violation: five days' suspension). And sure, she was aiding in the transport of stolen property (an Honor Code violation, as well as a violation of the Connecticut State Penal Code: so . . . prison time). But that wasn't the problem.

No, the real problem was that she had been caught with Fred Wright.

If she had been caught with someone else—

someone like, say, Hobson Crowe, or even Noah Percy—Sunday would probably have been able to weasel her way out of serious trouble. Yes, even under *these* sordid circumstances. She was a charmer, after all. Her dark, willowy good looks still counted for something, as did the Winthrop name. But Fred Wright's name counted for precisely squat. Besides, nobody was supposed to know that they were even on speaking terms anymore. Their relationship was supposed to be strictly clandestine—"straight up on the down low," as Hobson might say—because Fred was a guy whom certain parties (Sunday's parents, Allison Scott, Headmaster Olsen) saw as less than human, occupying a spot in the animal kingdom hierarchy somewhere between ill-behaved pets and show monkeys.

Very simply, *she was supposed to avoid him.*

Yet here they were.

Worse, they found themselves staring into the fat, froggy face of Mr. Burwell. If another teacher had caught them . . . but it was too late for "if."

Mr. Burwell looked pretty damn pleased with himself, sitting there in Fred's folding chair. And why wouldn't he? He'd pretty much told Fred that he hated his guts. He'd never bothered to learn the correct pronunciation of Sunday's name, which went a long way toward showing how he felt about *her*. Who knew how long he had waited for them in the dark, like some kind of deranged stalker?

Quel nightmare, as they say in France.

So. Sunday's life was about to take a serious turn for the worse. Definitely for the twisted. Because the final proverbial icing on the cake was that the stolen property—a small stack of personalized stationery—belonged to Headmaster Olsen. Only ten minutes ago, while stealing it, Sunday and Fred had learned something profoundly disturbing about its owner: namely, that Headmaster Olsen liked to watch homemade pornography.

But that was another story entirely.

"Isn't it ironical?" Mr. Burwell asked.

Sunday stared at him.

"Don't you think?" He leaned back in the chair. It creaked under his weight.

"I don't know," she answered, mostly because she didn't know what else to say. She knew she should have been afraid or apologetic or *something*. But frankly, all she felt was a strange curiosity about his wardrobe. Tonight's double-breasted suit was olive green, but . . . was it an Armani? No. There was no way a member of the Wessex faculty earned enough money to afford an Armani—not even a faculty member who had been around for twenty years, like Mr. Burwell. (Obviously, she wasn't judging Mr.

Burwell as a person based on his annual salary; she was just being realistic.) Yet she was positive she'd seen that exact suit in an Armani fall catalog. There was a certain quality, a sheen, which meant . . . *Oh, wait*. It was probably an *Emporio* Armani. As opposed to a Giorgio. Yes. Of course. Still stylish—even on a man of Mr. Burwell's carriage—but not quite as expensive.

"What's ironic?" Fred asked. He emphasized the second word, just a little.

Mr. Burwell's face soured. "That you kids think you're so much smarter than me. But I'm the one holding all the aces right now. Am I right?"

They were silent. Sunday stole a quick glance at Fred. He didn't look scared, either. In fact, he looked completely calm—and remarkably imposing, too, especially for somebody so tall and lanky. Her eyes lingered on his profile: the long neck, the tight jaw, the hawkish nose. He *was* cute, wasn't he? She'd had her doubts, but those were just due to years of ingrained elitism; as much as she hated to admit it, a postgraduate jock from some random family in Washington, D.C., didn't usually register on the AB radar. But then, that was the beauty of their odd little friendship. Or . . . was it more than friendship? Even after tonight, she still didn't know. That was the beauty, too: the intangible beauty of mystery.

"Am I right?" Mr. Burwell repeated.

Oh, will you please just shut up?

"Yes, you're right," Fred groaned. "So what's gonna happen to us?"

Mr. Burwell chuckled. His beady eyes hardened. "*I'm* asking the questions, Wright. First things first. Where were you two just now?"

Sunday bit her lip. She turned to Fred.

"We were messing around in the soccer fields." He lied without batting an eyelash. "It was my idea."

"Some nookie, eh?" Mr. Burwell leered at them. "I knew it. What else did you do? Blow a little rope to get yourself in the mood?"

Blow a little rope? Sunday almost laughed. She'd never heard that one before. It must have been an ancient drug reference—or maybe a combination of references that Mr. Burwell had mixed up. (Most teachers at Wessex, particularly the older ones, were about thirty years behind the times in terms of student slang. Headmaster Olsen had once asked Sunday—with a straight face—if she thought "grass was far out.") But at least Mr. Burwell didn't suspect that they were out raiding Olsen's mansion for subversive purposes.

"So what's gonna happen to us?" Fred asked again.

Mr. Burwell smiled. "Nothing," he said.

11

Sunday's jaw dropped. "What?" she cried.

"That's right. I'm not going to tell Olsen about this. You won't be getting in trouble."

"Why?" Fred asked.

Mr. Burwell laughed. "*Pah!* Because I'm gonna make a deal with you," he said.

Oh, God, no. Sunday felt sick. Something about the glint in his eye . . . he wasn't into pornography, too, was he? What if he wanted to blackmail them into making some kind of triple-X movie? *"Sex-Crazed Boarding-School Sluts From Hell."* What if the entire Wessex faculty was into filming students and watching them on cheap videotapes? After all, Headmaster Olsen had invited Winnie over to watch Noah Percy and some random woman . . . *ewww.* Sunday forced the thought from her mind. She couldn't go there again.

"I don't want to make a deal," Fred said. "I'd rather be punished."

Mr. Burwell arched an eyebrow. "I don't see as you have much of a choice," he said. "Unless you want to get expelled."

Sunday's pulse quickened. There it was. The word she'd secretly been dreading. *Expelled.* Until Mr. Burwell had actually said it, she hadn't thought she would crumble so easily. But now she knew she couldn't stand up to him. Better just to make the deal. She didn't want to get kicked out. Okay, yes, sometimes she fantasized about running away, about leaving Wessex forever, about cashing in her trust fund and settling in Bali or some other exotic locale and opening an upscale boutique or restaurant. But that was just a crazy dream. She couldn't deal with the consequences of facing her parents. Not over this. Not over anything real.

Besides, if Burwell involved Olsen right now, Olsen would know in an instant that she and Fred weren't returning from a late night make-out session. They looked like burglars. They *were* burglars. They had dressed all in black for the strict purpose of breaking into Olsen's house. Olsen's stationery was tucked into Fred's jacket. What if they had to empty their pockets?

"Well?" Burwell demanded.

"The deal," Sunday croaked. "Let's hear it."

Fred sighed. He sounded disappointed.

"It's four-pronged," Burwell said. "Meaning you do me four small favors, and I do you the very large favor of forgetting this unfortunate incident." He shifted in the chair and raised his forefinger. "Number one: You two are not to see each other outside my math class. Ever again. Do I make myself clear?"

"Yes." Sunday nodded. She tried not to look at Fred.

Mr. Burwell raised another finger. "B: You are to report any misbehavior directly to me. Meaning that if you catch anybody breaking the rules—and I mean *anybody*, be it Mackenzie Wilde or Hobson Crowe or even Allison Scott—you tell me about it. I don't care what it is. Drinking. Smoking. Blowing rope." He smiled. "Even curfew and coed visitation violations. Anything."

"You mean you want us to be your rats," Fred said.

"That's right." Mr. Burwell's smile vanished. He looked Fred directly in the eye. "I want you to be my rats. Because it takes a rat to catch a rat. This school is up to its ears in them, spoiled kids who like to think they can do whatever they want. They're wrong. The era of troublemaking is over. And I'm going to be the one who gets the credit for straightening things out." He took a deep breath. "And the third prong involves you, Wright. Just you. No more hanging out with Noah Percy. You're gonna hang out with the guys on the team. Winnie, Boyce, Carter, all the rest of them. You've got the exhibition game against Carnegie Mansion in less than two weeks, and I don't want to hear . . ."

Blood pounded in Sunday's temples. She couldn't listen to any more of this crap. All she wanted to do was to go back to her suite, back to her

14

tiny little room, and crawl into bed. She wanted the night to be over. She wanted to forget it, to pretend it never happened. Especially the part about the video. But one question kept nagging at her: Had Noah known that he was being filmed? Was he a willing participant in all this? She couldn't quite believe it. For one thing, the angle of the camera was really weird; he and the girl (whoever *she* was—another question altogether) had been shot from the floor, in one spot. As if the camera were hidden. And sure, Noah was a freak, but not enough of a freak to volunteer for pornography. His freakishness was a very specific brand of awkward, self-conscious—

"Winthorp!" Burwell barked.

She flinched. "Huh?"

"Answer me."

"Uh . . ." Sunday swallowed again. She glanced at Fred. He looked as if he were trying hard not to laugh. "What, um, was the question?"

"You're going to take care of number four. Right?"

"What . . . uh, number—"

"Your parents are going to help me sell my screenplay."

Sunday looked at him. "I'm sorry. What?"

"Have you been listening to a word I've said? My screenplay!" Mr. Burwell gestured wildly with his pudgy hands. "I know your father is a slick invest-ment type. Old money. And all those old-money guys know the Hollywood bigwigs. That's where they get *their* money."

"That's where . . ." Sunday didn't finish. Her mind drew a blank. *Screenplay. Hollywood. Old money.* There was no frame of reference, no possible way to respond. The conversation suddenly had nothing to do with getting busted. It had nothing to do with *anything*. Where was this coming from? Weren't they just talking about playing basketball against Carnegie Mansion?

Mr. Burwell glared at her. "You're telling me that your father doesn't know anyone in Hollywood? In the film industry?"

"I . . . I don't know," she whispered. She shook her head, baffled. Either she was already asleep and dreaming, or Mr. Burwell had gone completely insane. "Why would he—"

"You just tell your father to get me a meeting. Okay, Winthorp?"

"Win*throp*," she corrected automatically.

Burwell pushed himself to his feet. The folding chair screeched on the green linoleum. "And as for *you*, Wright . . ." He jabbed a chubby finger into Fred's chest. "I trust you will spend more time on the court. Got it?"

16

Fred didn't answer.

In that brief instant, Sunday caught Fred's eye. A wave of desperation washed over her, drowning out her anxiety over Mr. Burwell's deranged belief that her father could somehow get him a meeting with a "Hollywood bigwig." Was Fred mad at her for being a coward? Was he worried about his own fate? And what about their pact, the Manifesto of SAFU? Would it die with this evil bargain they were making with Burwell? Not that she had any intention of honoring it or meeting Burwell's ludicrous demands. But still. What did Fred *think* about all this? What were they going to *do*?

"Let's go, Winthorp," Mr. Burwell commanded her. He waved a hand toward the open doorway. "It's back to Reed Hall for you. Back to bed."

Fred stared at the floor.

"Now," Mr. Burwell growled.

Sunday shambled out of the room. She knew she wouldn't be getting any answers. Not here. It was a miserable ending to a miserable fiasco of a night—a night that by any standards had just started as some harmless boarding-school fun. But then, she should have known better than to try to have fun. That kind of urge hadn't gotten her very far in the past.

*   *   *

"Where have *you* been?" Allison hissed.

"I'm fine thanks, Al," Sunday answered dismally. "How are you?"

Allison's face darkened.

Sunday had been praying her suitemates would be asleep, or at least that Allison would be. No such luck. She stood in the doorway, teeth grinding, in all her J. Crew pajama glory. And Sunday had to hand it to the girl; even at this late hour, she still managed to look stunning: in full "Bizarro Kidman" form, as Fred liked to say—referring, of course, to the uncanny resemblance between Allison Scott and the former wife of Tom Cruise.

"Don't be mean, Al," Mackenzie called softly from inside the room. "I bet she's even more tired than we are. The moon is void-of-course, and Mars is retrograde—"

"Mackenzie!" Allison barked.

Sunday sighed. "Can't I just come in? I don't want to wake anyone up."

Allison shook her head and stepped aside. "Fine. Although I hope you know that you have some serious explaining to do. Mackenzie and I have been worried sick."

Right, Mother. At this point, Sunday only hoped Allison hadn't freaked and called Sunday's house, because then her mother really *would* be involved.

Tensions were running high enough. Sunday had promised everyone—her parents, Allison, even Mackenzie (although she was going to tell Mackenzie the truth eventually)—that she'd snapped out of this Fred Wright thing. No more sneaking out. No more causing trouble.

And now . . . well, now it was almost two-thirty in the morning.

"So?" Allison asked.

Sunday surveyed the suite's little common area. Once again, her mood sank to a new low. It was one thing to have to come home and have to answer to Allison. Yes, that was infuriating. Humiliating, even. But it was to be expected.

It was another thing entirely, however, to have to deal with Sven Larsen's interior design.

By hiring that Swedish vampire to strip their suite bare (Sunday didn't care how many would-be New York hipsters thought he was a genius), Allison had turned Sunday's home into a barren pit. A glimpse of hell. It didn't even look furnished. There was nothing here. Literally nothing . . . only a useless triangular black table and a black metal bench that had probably been inspired by some kind of medieval torture device. Poor Mackenzie had to spread out her star charts and astrology reference materials on the floor.

"Are you okay?" Mackenzie asked.

Sunday mustered a feeble smile.

"Of course she's okay," Allison grumbled.

Now *there* was the crucial difference between Mackenzie and Allison—right there, in a perfect little nutshell. Mackenzie was actually concerned about Sunday's well-being. Here she was, sprawled out in her own pj's amid a sea of books and papers. She had obviously been consulting the heavens to determine Sunday's fate. Now, maybe her methods were slightly misguided. Sunday wasn't one to judge. The point was that her intentions were sweet. Thoughtful. Sincere. Whereas Allison had only been concerned with potential scandal, with breaking the rules, with defying the "Wessex tradition." And what if Sunday *had* been in real trouble? What if she had been kidnapped? What if . . .

What if I had seen Noah Percy's naked body on a TV screen in Headmaster Olsen's house, then been forced to promise Mr. Burwell that my father would introduce him to film industry executives in Hollywood?

"Sunday?" Mackenzie prompted. "What happened?"

"I . . ." Sunday hesitated. She couldn't tell them the truth. First of all, they wouldn't believe it. Second, even if she tried, she would probably burst into tears. Or throw herself out a window. No, it was best just to keep all this madness to herself.

"Well?" Allison demanded impatiently. She

closed the suite door. "What's going on? Where were you? If you were out with that Fred person, Sunday, I swear—"

"Hey, can I ask you guys something?" Sunday interrupted. "Do either of you know anyone with Hollywood connections? Like, people whose parents would somehow be involved with the film business?"

Allison's face shriveled like a prune. "What? *Why*?"

"Ooh, I know of somebody!" Mackenzie said. "Well, he's not here anymore. But that guy, you know . . . he was a senior when we were sophomores; he was friends with Salvatore Viverito." She snapped her fingers. "Carl something. No. Carl, Carl—"

"Carlton," Allison mumbled between clenched teeth. "Carlton Douglas."

"Exactly!" Mackenzie beamed at Sunday. "Carlton Douglas. Remember? His father was in charge of Universal. Or Paramount, I think."

"Yeah . . . Carlton," Sunday said. An image of a nebbishy kid with horn-rimmed glasses flashed through her mind. "I do remember. He was always talking about 'the business'—trying to sound mysterious, like we didn't know what he meant. And he—"

"Um, *excuse* me?" Allison snapped. "Hel-*lo*?"

"What?" Sunday said. "This is important."

Allison glared at her. Then she marched to her

own room and slammed the door. Sunday winced. She turned to Mackenzie again. But Mackenzie was nodding to herself, staring off into space, her brown eyes oblivious.

"Remember the way Carlton used to talk about classes?" she mused. "Like they were movies? I took Twentieth-Century European History with him. I remember this one time—it was the first day of class, and he was like, 'This is a good course.'" She deepened her voice, imitating him. "'Very graphic. Very *Band of Brothers* meets *American Masters*.'"

"He was probably trying to hit on you," Sunday said dryly.

"You think?" Mackenzie stretched and yawned. "Wow. You know, I would have fooled around with him. Back then, anyway. He was pretty cute, wasn't he?"

"Oh, yeah," Sunday said. "Very Woody Allen meets Haley Joel Osment."

Mackenzie stuck her tongue out at her. Then she smiled. "Just for that, you're going to have to tell me where you were just now."

"I . . . I . . ." Sunday's nausea suddenly returned, as if she'd just caught a whiff of expired milk. Something occurred to her right then, and it was more terrifying than anything else she had witnessed or pondered tonight: *This may be the last time I ever get to hang out with Mackenzie like this.* Their years of carefree joking around and teasing each other were coming to an end. No doubt about it. Sunday was living a lie right now, *several* lies. For all she knew, Mr. Burwell had been lying, too. He might have already gone to Headmaster Olsen. He might have already called Sunday's parents. Expulsion papers might have already been drafted. She shuddered. How the hell had she even gotten into this situation?

"I'm just kidding, Sun," Mackenzie soothed. "You can tell me tomorrow."

"I know." A lump formed in Sunday's throat. She nodded. "Thanks, Mack." Her voice caught. She averted her eyes and hurried to her room, closing the door behind her. For a second, she leaned against it. Her breath came fast.

What now?

Well, she couldn't have a breakdown; Mackenzie would hear her crying. No, she had to distract herself. She had to take action. She had to . . . *I'll write Fred a letter.* Perfect. She would tell him exactly how she felt (if she could figure that out). More importantly, she would ask him how *he* felt. She sniffed and wiped her bloodshot eyes, then sat at her desk and grabbed a piece of computer paper from the printer. Yes. This was what she had to do. She clicked a ballpoint pen and began to write, even before her thoughts were fully formed:

Dear Fred,

Wow. Some night, huh? It reminds me of that joke from the second grade. You remember:

"That was so funny I forgot to laugh."

Okay. Maybe not. I'm just trying to use lame humor as a defense mechanism. Noah says I do that sometimes. I mean, I don't want to think about what's happened, much less write about it. But I have to be honest with you, Fred. I'm scared. I think that's a first for me. The last time I came close to being scared was when I spilled Frappuccino on a blouse I borrowed from my mother without permission.

Wait—I told you I was pathetic, didn't I? Well, if I didn't, I'm telling you now.

What do you think was going on at Olsen's house? What were those guys doing? I mean, I know what they were doing. Headmaster Olsen and Winnie were watching a porn movie starring Noah Percy. I always knew that Winnie was screwed up, but I never thought he was a sick pervert. And what about Olsen? Is his life too short on drama? I guess quoting Shakespeare just doesn't cut it anymore. Then there's the question of the mystery woman. Who is she? I'd put her at about twenty-five years old. Too old to be a student, I think. Mind you, I'm basing this on

24

a blurry shot of her butt. Butt-shots aren't exactly reliable.

On an entirely unrelated note, how do you think Mr. Burwell is able to afford that suit?

So. As you can tell, my thoughts are scattered, and I'm pretty much vomiting words onto the page, writing about as fast as I can think. My wrist is starting to hurt. I'll try to keep it short.

I think we should chill for a while. Maybe we should put the Manifesto of SAFU on the back burner until we figure this stuff out. I don't want to get kicked out of here, Fred. I mean, I'm sick of playing this stupid role and getting stomped all over by people who are supposed to be my friends, but on the other hand . . .

Jesus. Now I sound like an ad for one of those on-line support groups.

Basically, what I'm saying is . . . well, I don't know what I'm saying.

What do you think? What do you want to do? Should we talk to Noah about this? I know he thinks you're like the coolest guy on the planet. We need to know if HE knows what's going on.

Write back—
Sunday

The pen clattered to Sunday's desk. There was a cramp in her wrist. She shook out her hand. Tears welled in her eyes. A few drops fell to the page, smudging the words "support groups." Funny. She almost laughed out loud. She'd tried to write this letter for the express purpose of avoiding a breakdown, and here she was, weeping like a child.

Now *that* was "ironical."

Memo From Coach Watts to All Students on the Boys' Varsity Basketball Team

To: The Wessex Warriors (V)
From: Coach Watts
Date: 10/3
Re: Carnegie Mansion Exhibition Game

All right, ladies. It's showtime again. The annual Carnegie Mansion Exhibition Game is right around the corner. And this time, I'm employing a new strategy.

It's called the No Respect Plan. The three rules are as follows:

* Play hard. Even if you're on the bench, I want to see sweat.

* Play fair. No flagrant fouls, no tripping, no wedgies. (That means you, Boyce.)

* Play mean. You want to shake somebody's hand after the game? Then I better not see your sorry behind on my bus.

We've lost to Carnegie Mansion every year for the past twelve. Anyone know why? Because there was no fire. You want to play nice, go back home to Chump City. I don't want wimps. I want winners. This year we're going to take back the victory—on Carnegie's home court, in front of all the parents, all the alumni, all the college scouts who don't get a chance to see you play during the regular season. It's not a question of "if." It's a question of "by how many points."

Do I make myself clear, ladies? It's our time now.

And let me just say, for the record, that I'm proud of you. Since the Tony Viverito incident, nobody's gotten in trouble. Nice work. So buckle down for the next week. Practice hard, practice fair, and practice mean. Don't screw this up.

See you tomorrow afternoon at the gym for the first practice. 3:30 sharp. GO, WARRIORS!

cc: Phillip Olsen

2

From the time he was eight years old, Noah Percy had always secretly imagined that there was a sound track to his life. He could pinpoint the exact moment it had started, in fact. It was the very first time he'd heard "Sympathy for the Devil" by the Rolling Stones. His nanny (a kind, doughy Englishwoman named Liza) had absently popped the song into the CD player while preparing him for school, and by the time the bus showed up, the hypnotic, train-whistle chorus of *"Woo-wooo! . . . Woo-wooo! . . . Woo-wooo!"* had permanently embedded itself in Noah's brain. He sang *"woo-wooo"* for the entire forty-five-minute ride to Fenwick Elementary—over and over again, mostly at the top of his lungs, ignoring the pleas of the driver and fellow students to shut up, for the love of God, or they would stuff his book bag down his throat and toss his body out on the road. He spent the rest of the morning in the principal's office.

Anyway, since that momentous occasion, the music had never stopped—although he rarely sang along again. No, from then on, the sound track was for him, and him alone. Wherever he went, he was accompanied by invisible speakers, blasting inaudible songs at all the crucial turning points in *The Noah Percy Saga, Part I.* This was no ordinary film, after all. It was a rich, tragic, comic epic—the Hollywood term for the genre was "dramedy"—and as such, it deserved an epic score. A preview might include these highlights:

1) *Scene:* The second-floor bathroom, Logan Hall. MR. WENDT catches NOAH tossing a firecracker into a urinal.
Song: "Oops! I Did It Again" (Britney Spears)

2) *Scene:* An illicit party at WINNIE's New York City brownstone. The first time Noah ever gets drunk. HOBSON CROWE forces him to drink piña coladas until he barfs all over a genuine Louis XIV chaise lounge.
Song: "Escape: The Piña Colada Song" (Artist unknown, some '70s guy)

3) *Scene*: MISS BURKE'S faculty apartment, three nights ago. The first and only time Noah ever has sex. He surrenders his virginity to Miss Burke on her moth-eaten sofa.
Song: "Loser" (Beck)

Actually, that last track was fast becoming Noah's theme song. It had pretty much kicked in the moment the scene was over and had only intermittently fallen silent since then—usually when he went to the bathroom. It would have been nice if a different song could have marked such a pivotal rite of passage: something more inspirational and confident, like "Hot for Teacher" by Van Halen. But no. Noah wasn't worthy of such material.

And now, lying here in his bed after another sleepless night—staring up at the ceiling, incapacitated, nauseated—Noah couldn't deny that the music was fitting. He *was* a loser. Only a loser would have done what he did. Only a loser would have sex with a drunken, unbalanced teacher—a *crazy* woman—just because, well . . . for obvious reasons. And now he was late for breakfast, and soon he would be late for class. But why bother getting up? He didn't have an appetite. He was in no mood for phony chitchat or Allison Scott's grinding teeth. He definitely couldn't BS his way through Miss Burke's lecture. He couldn't bear to face her. He hadn't even cracked the book he was supposed to read. He didn't even know what book it *was*—

There was a knock on the door.

A visitor. Wonderful. Noah turned to the alarm clock on his bedside table. It wasn't even nine o'clock yet. This was private time. *His* time. But there was never really any private time at boarding school, was there?

"Hey, Noah! Open up, dude!"

Noah rubbed his eyes. "Winnie? Is that you?"

"Yeah. Come on." The doorknob rattled.

"What are you . . ." Noah pushed himself out of bed and staggered through several days' worth of unwashed shirts, then flicked the lock.

"Whassup?" Winnie burst into the room, nearly barreling Noah over. He looked very happy. A lot happier than Noah, anyway. A wide smile was pasted onto his pudgy face. Even his outfit was strangely . . . gay. (Not gay meaning same-sex oriented, but gay in the original sense of the word: ebullient, joyous.) Normally, Winnie was a khakis-and-oxford-shirt kind of guy. But today he was wearing a bright red sweater and yellowish cords that almost matched the color of his hair. It was mildly unsettling.

"What do you want?" Noah asked.

"For chrissakes, Percy, put some pants on."

Noah glanced down at himself. He was naked except for a pair of Wessex Academy boxer shorts. He sighed, then hobbled over to the dresser.

"Man, you really lucked out this year, huh?" Winnie said. He slumped down at Noah's desk and glanced around the room. "I forgot how huge this place was."

"Yeah, well, the trade-off is having Burwell as a dorm advisor," Noah muttered. He wriggled into some sweatpants, then pulled a T-shirt over his head. "So, Winnie, uh . . . not to be a dick or anything, but what are you doing here?"

Winnie raised his fuzzy eyebrows. "What do you think?"

"Well, either you want to sell me some notebooks at an inflated price, or you want to get me addicted to chewing tobacco. The going rate is five bucks a tin, right?"

"That's funny, dude," Winnie said. "Anybody ever tell you that you are a funny guy?"

Noah gave his old pal a big, fake smile. "Nope. Nobody. Oh, wait. *You* have. About four million times. Since we were six years old. So why are you here, again?"

"I want to know about you and Miss Burke," Winnie said.

At that moment, Noah experienced a very unpleasant sensation—something akin to being tossed off a roof. His head spun. His stomach rose to his throat. There was no way Winnie could know about him and Miss Burke. None at all. Unless Miss Burke had told somebody. But why would she do that? She'd lose her job, get arrested, go to prison, become some evil lesbian convict's personal slave . . . *but wait!* Winnie had been her messenger. *The note.* Yes, Winnie had seen what she'd written to Noah: the strange apology, the open invitation to her house. Maybe he'd guessed that something had happened. But no, nobody in a million years would ever guess that Miss Burke had seduced Noah Percy. Miss Burke was twenty-two and looked like a model. Noah was seventeen and didn't. He looked like a beanpole with a tuft of curly hair. It was simply too preposterous. Noah hardly believed it himself, and he'd *been* there.

"Well?" Winnie said. "What happened that night?"

"Why? Do you have another note from her?"

Winnie shook his head. "Nope. I'm just curious. That's all."

"Like I told you, we talked about the summer reading," Noah said weakly. *"Nineteen Eighty-Four."* His knees wobbled. He leaned against the dresser for support, then quickly straightened. "And . . . uh, well, that led to, um, a broader conversation about political fiction in general, with an emphasis on totalitarian themes—"

"Dude? I'm not in the mood for one of your stupid little rants. They're boring."

Noah scowled. "Yeah? So? The conversation I had with Miss Burke was boring. And why are you so curious about it?" His voice rose. He figured indignation was his best strategy. "Frankly, it's none of your goddamn business."

"'Frankly, it's none of your goddamn business,'" Winnie echoed in a childish, singsong voice. "Well, well. Touchy, aren't we?"

Noah glared at him. "Don't you have somewhere to be right now? Shouldn't you be in class or ripping someone off?"

Winnie shrugged. "I have first period free."

There was another knock on the door.

"Expecting someone?" Winnie asked.

"No," Noah said. For some reason, he felt sicker than ever. It couldn't be somebody like . . . well, Miss Burke. Not at this hour. Could it?

"Hello? Anybody home?"

It wasn't Miss Burke. It was a man. Noah didn't recognize the voice.

"Who is it?" Noah called.

"UPS. I have a package here for Noah Percy."

Noah turned to Winnie again. Winnie shrugged. Normally, packages went to the mailroom at the Student Activities Center. So. A direct delivery probably meant that some lame prank was afoot. Probably care of Winnie himself. The kid simply loved to get on people's nerves, didn't he? Just last week he'd short-sheeted some poor sophomore's bed for being late on a tobacco payment. What fun! Yes, this was exactly what Noah needed, given his current state of mental health. The timing couldn't be better.

"Can you sign for this, please?" the voice demanded impatiently.

"Why not?" Noah trudged to the door and threw it open.

His eyes narrowed.

It *was* a UPS guy. Either that or somebody who had rented a UPS uniform. Everything looked legitimate: the brown polyester pants, the official patch, the slender cardboard box tucked under his arm— even the annoyed look on his craggy old face. He thrust the box into Noah's hands, then held out an electronic clipboard and pen.

"Sign here, please."

Noah just stared at him.

"Preferably some time this week," the guy said.

"Oh. Sorry." Noah grabbed the pen and hastily scrawled his signature on the little computer pad. "Thanks."

"Percy, right?" the guy grunted. He glanced from the pad to Noah's face. "P-e-r-c-y?"

"Yeah."

"Great. Have a nice day, kid." He started punching letters into the keypad, then turned and vanished down the hall.

"What is it?" Winnie asked.

Noah glanced down at the box. It was about the size and shape of a book, but it didn't weigh that much. There was no return address.

"I have no idea," he mumbled, closing the door.

"Well, open it, dude!"

"Now?"

Winnie grinned. "Preferably some time this week," he said, sounding pleased.

All at once, Noah felt a strong urge to punch Winnie in the face. He wasn't sure where it had come from or why it was so violent. He'd felt similar urges before, of course, to a lesser degree. Many times. But this was different. Maybe it had something to do with the way Winnie was just *sitting* there—for no good reason at all, in *Noah's* room, ordering *Noah* around, wearing a tight red sweater that accentuated his flabby breasts . . . as though he belonged there. And he didn't.

"If I open this, do you promise to get lost immediately?" Noah asked.

"Open the freaking box, Noah."

Noah sighed. To remove Winnie, he'd have to use force, and the bastard was just too damn big. Best just to open the stupid package and get this over with. He sat down on his bed and ripped apart the cardboard—ferociously, as if he were a famine victim and there were chocolate cake inside. Pieces of white Styrofoam popcorn fell all over his mattress.

It was a videotape.

"What is it?" Winnie asked.

"I don't know," Noah said. There was no label, but a small piece of folded white paper was Scotch-taped to one side. Noah tore it off and unfolded it.

We're taking this to the administration if you do not comply with our demands. Arrange for the transfer of $200,000 to this account: 077-GR626511-03, Federated Bank of Georgetown, Cayman Islands. To access, phone 011-596-266-3117. Ask for "M." The password is "Ophelia." We suggest using your trust fund. How you get the money is not our problem. You have two weeks.

Ha, ha, ha. Noah shook his head. He knew it. Good old Winnie. He really took it to the extreme, didn't he? The UPS guy was an especially nice touch. So was the line about "suggesting" the trust fund. Winnie knew damn well that Noah couldn't touch the money his parents had squirreled away for him. On the other hand, the Cayman Islands bit . . . Winnie probably could have been a little more creative than that. Nobody talked about laundering money in the Cayman Islands anymore.

That was a late-'90s B-movie kind of crime, at best.

"Well?" Winnie prodded. "What's it say?"

"See for yourself," Noah muttered. He crumpled the note into a little ball and tossed it to him. "Looks like I'm in big trouble."

Winnie's eyes flashed over the piece of paper. He laughed once.

"So, Winnie, old buddy," Noah said dully. "Can I borrow two hundred thousand bucks? Just for a little while. I'm good for it. I promise."

"Funny, funny," Winnie said. He dropped the note to the floor. "Well?"

"Well, what?"

"Don't you want to see what's on that tape?"

Noah gave him a blank stare. "I know what's on it. A few tasty shots of you mooning me or giving me the finger."

Winnie frowned. "What?"

"Forget it." Noah flopped back down on the bed and stared at the ceiling. Once again, the faint strains of "Loser" were creeping into his mind. That was the cue. The scene was over. Time for Winnie to make his grand exit.

"You don't want to watch it?" Winnie asked.

"No. So can you go now? Please?"

"Are you kidding?" Winnie jumped out of the chair and snatched the tape off the bed.

Noah bolted upright. "Hey!" he barked. Now he was genuinely pissed. "I'm serious. Get out of here. I mean it. Take the tape if you want, but get out."

Winnie shook his head and crouched in front of the trunk, where Noah's TV-VCR unit was perched. "I can't, dude," he said. "My VCR's broken. And I gotta see this thing."

"So go to the Audio-Visual Center," Noah pleaded. "The tape's yours, anyway, isn't it?"

But Winnie didn't answer. He had already shoved the tape into the slot. Now *this* was an outrage. One of the few reasons Noah had looked forward to his final year at Wessex was for the express purpose of being able to watch videotapes—ones that *he* had chosen—alone. It was one of the fringe benefits of being a senior: Only seniors were allowed to have TVs or VCRs in their rooms. For three long years Noah had waited for this—for *this*!—imagining how cool it would be to come home after a hard day of classes and flip on MTV or the Playboy Channel, or to rent smutty movies from the New Farmington Blockbuster. And what did he get? Winslow Ellis and an ill-conceived prank. At nine in the morning.

"Here we go," Winnie announced. He turned on the TV and pushed the play button.

A blast of white noise exploded from the speaker.

"Jesus!" Noah shouted. He cupped his hands over

his ears. Static filled the screen. "Turn it *down*! You have to put it on channel three! Channel—"

"Got it," Winnie yelled back. He jabbed at the buttons.

The volume shrank. An image appeared.

Noah leaned forward. The picture was fuzzy. What *was* this? It looked really cheap: black-and-white and . . .

He jerked back, panicking. *No*—

"Hey, man," Winnie mumbled. "Is that you?"

This is impossible. Noah shook his head. He felt as if his vital organs had been dumped into a Cuisinart. There were two people on screen. A guy and a girl. No, a boy and a *woman*. Peeling off each other's clothes. On a ratty couch next to a makeshift plywood coffee table—

"Holy . . ." Winnie didn't finish.

Noah flung himself off the bed and lunged for the TV, simultaneously toppling over Winnie and smashing his hand into the power button.

"Hey!" Winnie yelled.

The TV went dead.

Noah tumbled to the floor. He was panting. His heart pounded. He had to think. But he couldn't. Horror made thinking impossible. Except . . . *get rid of the tape.* Yes. Smash it to pieces. Pretend it never existed. Burn the note and the UPS box. Maybe kill Winnie, too. Right. No witnesses. Winnie was long overdue for an untimely death, anyway.

He froze.

Winnie was laughing.

Unbelievable. The son-of-a-bitch actually thought this was funny. He was kneeling there in front of the TV, doubled over, cackling. . . . Of all the affronts Noah had ever suffered in his life, *this* . . . okay. Enough. Without thinking, he seized Winnie's fleshy neck and squeezed.

"Hey!" Winnie gasped. His eyes bulged. "Get off of me!"

"Then shut the hell up," Noah growled.

Winnie nodded. His face started to turn red.

Oh, brother. Noah let him go. Attacking Winnie was shameful. More importantly, it didn't make him feel any better. He pushed himself to his feet and ran a hand through his curls. *Relax!* he ordered himself. But that didn't work, either. No, right now, only a hefty dose of animal tranquilizer or a full-body massage could possibly do the trick. He started pacing across the laundry-strewn linoleum. What did he know for sure? Well, nothing, really. Except that he was perfectly, royally, majorly screwed.

"Hey, Noah," Winnie said. He grinned. "I didn't realize you were so, uh, *passionate* about the summer reading."

Noah whirled and glared at him. "You know, when somebody tries to strangle you, that's generally a sign that they don't want you around."

Winnie shrugged, then stood and smoothed his rumpled clothing. "Right. One thing, though. You said you had a boring conversation with Miss Burke." He sat back down at the desk. "If that's boring, I'd be curious to see what you think an exciting conversation looks like."

For a few seconds, rage prevented Noah from replying. "Why did you *do* this?" he finally shrieked. "Why did you videotape me with Miss—"

"Whoa, hold on a sec," Winnie interrupted. "You think *I* was the one who did this?"

"Who else?"

"Why would I?"

"Because you're a sick bastard?" Noah guessed.

Winnie looked Noah in the eye. "I had nothing to do with this, Noah. Come on, dude. I'm your friend."

Noah just stared at him. "I . . . I can't believe this," he mumbled. He sat back down on his bed and buried his face in his hands. "I can't freaking *believe this*!"

"What?"

"Get out of here, Winnie."

Winnie let out a deep breath. "Whatever, Noah. Believe what you want. I'm trying to help you. And, not to be a jerk, but you look like you could use some help."

Noah glanced up. "How can *you* help *me*?" he spat.

"I made six figures manipulating the stock market

last year. Remember? If these people are serious—and it looks like they are—I can teach you how to make that two hundred grand in two weeks, no problem."

Now it was Noah's turn to laugh. "You honestly expect me to believe that?"

"You honestly expect me to believe that you had sex with Miss Burke?" Winnie asked.

Hmm. Point well taken.

"I'm sorry," Winnie said, softening his tone. "I shouldn't have laughed. I feel bad for you. Really. It's just that I can help you. I mean, do you think my operation stopped when they caught me with the pump-and-dump last year? Come on. I'm smarter than that. That was the tip of the iceberg. I've doubled my profits since then." He winked. "I even have my own offshore account. You can have one, too."

Blood began to boil in Noah's veins. That wink. Winnie looked so smug. So goddamn proud of himself. For being an extortionist sleazebag, for *stealing* from people. *If* he was telling the truth. The whole thing was beyond absurd; it was unfathomable.

"Look, Noah, it's just really lucky that I'm here," Winnie said. "Because now that I know about this, I can help you. I can teach you how to make money."

Noah didn't reply. It *was* really lucky, wasn't it? Extraordinarily lucky. Unbelievably lucky. Winnie had just happened to stroll by for an early morning visit—

"Hey, whaddya know, I think I'll say hi to Noah!"—the moment the
package arrived. Yes, it was almost as convenient as being
asked to hand-deliver Miss Burke's note. For all Noah
knew, Winnie might be the only other person involved,
besides Miss Burke. But in a way, it didn't matter. Because
Winnie was still right. Noah *did* need help. Desperately.
Regardless of who was pulling the strings here, Noah
couldn't let the administration see that tape. Period.
And if that meant paying off Winnie . . . well, then that's
what he would have to do. He could already hear the
sound track for this scene ("Help!" by the Beatles) kicking in at full volume.

"Will you let me help you?" Winnie asked.

"Sure," Noah said. "One minor thing, though.
Well, actually, a couple of little details. What if I *can't*
come up with the two hundred grand? How am I gonna
keep Headmaster Olsen and my parents from finding
out that I was filmed having sex with a teacher?"

Winnie sighed. "I told you. It won't be a problem.
Trust me."

"I'd sooner trust Satan," Noah said.

"Yeah, well, Satan isn't here. And I am." Winnie
flashed another confident smile. "So it looks like
we're stuck together, huh?"

Noah smiled back. He felt like death.

HE-E-ELP!

From: Undisclosed Sender
To: Undisclosed Recipient
Subject: Phase Two

NP fell like a domino. Has no idea who is
involved, except PB2. All set to proceed; no
need to involve the parents.

From: Undisclosed Sender
To: Undisclosed Recipient
Subject: re: Phase Two

Excellent. You know, you were right all
along. The fewer people involved, the better
off we all are. More profit down the line,
less mess. But are you certain the risk
factor for Phase Three is minimal?

From: Undisclosed Sender
To: Undisclosed Recipient
Subject: re: re: Phase Two

Absolutely. Why did we choose NP in the
first place? He'll do anything to stay at
Wessex, and nobody can BS as well as he can.
He's perfect. Also, this time I won't be
directly involved. In case there are any
problems, all paths will lead to NP. If
you're nervous, though, you should have a
backup plan. It's always good to cover your
bases. You taught me that.

```
From: Undisclosed Sender
To: Undisclosed Recipient
Subject: re: re: re: Phase Two
```

I'm not too worried about covering our
bases. Have you forgotten the exhibition
game against CM? It's going to be a good
year, my boy.

Fred's Response to Sunday

Hey Sunday,

I got your note. Don't worry about anything, okay? Burwell can't push us around. He's a burnt-out, bitter old freak. He actually thinks he can salvage his noncareer by recruiting rats to bust "troublemakers." YOU hold the aces. Not him. You're an AB. A player. A third-generation Winthrop. The school DEPENDS on you. I mean, what's the worst that can happen? You get suspended? Come on! That's a five-day vacation. A trip home. A sweet deal, if you ask me.

By the way, Burwell never found the stationery. I still have it.

Don't you see? Olsen and Winnie don't know that we caught them. As soon as we figure out what they're doing, we'll go public. We'll change the school. Forever. Just like we promised in the Manifesto. On a massive scale. This is war! Today's swine is tomorrow's sausage! Think about it. Do you know how big a deal this is? It's headline material. It's the stuff TV movies are made of. Headmasters and pornography. Scandal. Voyeurism. I mean, this is up there with devil worship and mass orgies and snuff films.

Anyway, I agree: We have to find out if Noah knows the truth. We also have to get Winnie alone and find out what he knows. And if he doesn't want to talk, I'll scare the facts out of him. I'll pummel that cow-hearted sack of lard if I have to. It would be a pleasure. We'll ruin these bastards.

48

Above all, we have to get that tape. That's the key. If you want, I'll handle that part of it myself. But that's what we have to do. By any means necessary. I'm sorry if this sounds pushy or violent or fanatical, but you wanted to know how I feel, and I'm telling you. Personally, I'm getting a weird kick out of all this. Is that bad?

Don't be scared. I won't let you down.

Fred

P.S. How much does Burwell's suit actually cost?

3

It wasn't until lunchtime—when he spotted Noah in the cafeteria line, looking like a disheveled homeless person—that Fred Wright was finally able to breathe a sigh of relief. Sort of. At least he could lay to rest the fear that Noah had split campus for good. Until then, Fred had been almost sure of it. He'd been all over the place: Noah's room, the library, even the Waldorf, that sour snob-hole in the woods . . . and after a while, he couldn't help but draw the grim conclusion: *Noah Percy's gone AWOL.* The kid's sanity was precarious enough. Fred had known *that* long before he'd seen any seamy footage of Noah and some mystery chick doing the nasty.

The funny thing, of course, was that Noah's insanity was what Fred dug about him the most: that oddball, lunatic self-absorption—the way he was poised to freak out at any second and analyze his behavior at the same time. Well, that and his love of dinosaur classic rock bands. And his massive CD collection. And the fact that he'd never made any assumptions about Fred, unlike almost every other kid at Wessex—all the brats who'd pegged him as a jock, an idiot who'd been plucked from a crappy public school for the sole purpose of saving their basketball team. Which, to a large degree, was true. But still. Nobody likes to be pigeonholed.

"Yo, Noah!" Fred yelled. He cupped his hands around his mouth. "Noah Percy!"

Noah didn't answer.

Fred shoved his way through the lunchtime crowd, ignoring the curious stares of the other students. As usual, the dining hall was packed and frantic at this hour. Almost everybody seemed to be looking at Fred—except Noah, who was gazing down at his empty tray, completely lost in space. If Fred didn't know any better, he'd have said that Noah was stoned.

"Earth to Noah!" he called.

Still nothing.

"Noah!"

Only when Fred poked him in the shoulder did Noah finally lift his head.

"Oh," he said. "Hey, man."

Fred tried to smile. "Uh . . . where's the blazer?" he asked.

Noah blinked. His skin was the color of chalk, except for the purple bags under his eyes. "Huh?"

"That tweed blazer you always wear." Fred eyed Noah's peculiar getup. "You're not usually a sweatpants and T-shirt kind of guy."

"Yeah." Noah lifted his shoulders. "Well."

"What about the dress code?"

"What about it?" Noah said.

"Haven't teachers given you any flak today? You know, for being so casual?"

"I haven't been to class yet."

"You *haven't*?" Fred gasped. "But—"

"No butting," a shrill voice snapped behind them.

Fred turned around. He was expecting to see an uptight chick, but he found himself glaring down at a boy who looked no older than twelve. The kid's neck was roughly the same circumference as a baseball bat. He stared up at Fred defiantly, clutching his empty lunch tray in front of his puny chest like a shield.

"What did you say?" Fred asked.

"No butting," the kid repeated. He jerked his head over his shoulder. "The line starts back there."

"But—"

"But nothing. We're all in this together, dude. And I got here first."

Fred stared at him. Then he smiled. He'd always had a soft spot for wiseasses. And this obnoxious twerp actually made Fred *think.* Yes, with that irritating little remark, he'd somehow reminded Fred of what he'd forgotten to articulate in his letter to Sunday: *We're all in this together, dude.* It was true, very true—every single student at Wessex was in the same rocky, depraved, whacked-out boat. Fred included. He should have made that more clear. In the letter, he'd sort of placed himself above everyone else; he'd made himself out to be the hero, the one who would save Wessex from its own sins. *Fred Wright, to the rescue!* Bad call. He didn't even feel that way. He didn't have a messiah complex. At least, not that he knew of. Had he freaked Sunday out? Had he made her uncomfortable? Now he was worried that he'd come off sounding like some kind of demented, one-man militia. . . .

"You know what, Fred?" Noah mumbled. "You can have my place in line. I'm not really all that hungry." He handed over his tray, then turned and shuffled toward the exit. "Later."

"No, wait." Fred passed off the tray to the kid and dashed after Noah. "I'm not hungry, either." He ran up alongside him. "What do you say you come join me for a dip?"

"I don't dip."

"I know," Fred said.

"Oh," Noah said. "Right."

Fred laughed uncomfortably. Dipping—and the fact that it made Noah barf—was a favorite inside joke between them. And now Noah had forgotten that they'd even *talked* about it? Something was very wrong here.

"Hey, man," Fred said. "Are you sure you're all right?"

"I'm fine," Noah said. He pushed through the double doors without bothering to hold them. They nearly slammed in Fred's face. But Fred doggedly pressed forward. He chased Noah out into the early fall sunshine.

"Wait up!" Fred called.

Noah didn't slow down. He sped to a trot, hurrying across the plush green quad in the direction of their dorm—right past Hobson Crowe and a group of other ABs, a bunch of blond clones whom Fred barely recognized: Boyce and Carter and Sutton or whatever.

"Yo, dawg!" Hobson cried. He flashed some kind of ghetto hand signal as Noah ran by. "The sweatpants look is *fresh*, yo! I'm down wit' dat!"

The other ABs laughed.

For chrissakes . . . Fred broke into a run. He darted past them and managed to sprint in front of Noah, then whirled around to cut him off.

"Come on, man," he panted. "I gotta talk to you."

"About what?" Noah said.

Fred opened his mouth. A second later, he closed it.

That was a good question. About what? About how Fred had watched a videotape of Noah having sex? And how exactly would he broach that delicate subject? Maybe he should think this through some more. But no, he couldn't back off, because this wasn't just about Noah. It was about *him*, too. It was about the guilt that still clung to him like a mildewed blanket: the guilt over Tony Viverito. *That* was why Fred had been so gung ho in his response to Sunday's letter. *That* was why he was so hell-bent on tearing this place apart and exposing the truth, whatever the truth might be. And that was why he couldn't let Noah go right now. In some strange, convoluted way, it all came back to the tin of Old Hickory in Tony Viverito's book bag. The tin that had been planted there. The tin that had gotten Tony expelled.

The thing was, Fred knew that he shouldn't even give a crap. *He* hadn't framed Tony Viverito. Besides, Tony was no friend of Fred's. He'd told Fred to go screw himself on more than one occasion. He was a lousy basketball player, too. The Wessex Warriors were better off without him. And the real clincher was that he was Salvatore Viverito's little brother: Salvatore, Diane's once and future boyfriend, the cheesy schmuck who had stolen her away from Fred and plunged his senior year into a downward spiral of misery.

But still, somehow, Fred couldn't help but obsess

over Tony's fate. Or at least be outraged by it. Regardless of his family, Tony had gotten the boot—his life had been *ruined*—for one simple, heinous reason: Mr. Burwell had hoped to scare Fred. That was it. That was how freaking *cold* this place was. And that meant Fred was somewhat responsible, whether he wanted to be or not. He could just picture the pronouncement, too: *Fred Wright must learn to fear us, and we can use Tony Viverito to that end because he is expendable.*

It had probably gone down like this: Mr. Burwell (or whoever it was; Fred was pretty sure it was Burwell, anyway) had planted the dip on Tony just to prove to Fred that the administration could mess with anyone at any time. And the most ridiculous part of all was that Tony Viverito didn't even *dip*, because it made him barf, just like Noah. . . . Well, there was no point in rehashing the whole theory again. Because in the end, that was all it was: a theory. Fred had no proof that Mr. Burwell was the one who'd done it. And he'd wasted far too much time stewing over all this—mostly because Tony believed that *Fred* was the one who'd framed him. The tobacco in his bag had been Old Hickory: Fred's brand. Burwell had probably planned it that way.

Twisted. Very, very twisted.

But the past couldn't be changed. What was done was done. Anyway, it had nothing to do with Noah and *his* problems. Not directly. Although it did have to do with the fact that the people who ran this school were an evil bunch of crooks and sociopaths and deviants. . . .

"Look, man," Noah muttered. "If you're just gonna stand there, let me go. I got things to do, all right?"

"Headmaster Olsen has a videotape of you having sex," Fred blurted.

Noah blinked. His skin turned visibly pale. "What?" he croaked.

Fred nodded, swallowing. The sun was very hot, beating down on his tousled hair. Nice one. Yeah, real tactful. He felt like punching himself. Whatever. He couldn't dawdle anymore. Maybe it wasn't the most sensitive approach, but at the very least, he had Noah's attention now.

"You're full of it," Noah said.

"No. I'm not."

Noah looked away. "Well, I—I, um, I have no idea what you're talking about."

Fred began to feel queasy. A two-year-old could tell that Noah was lying right now. Which meant . . . *He knows about the tape.* But what else did it mean? That he'd been a willing participant? No way. Somebody must have secretly filmed Noah, then told him about it—maybe threatened him in some way. That was the only possible explanation. Something about the way

Noah had behaved on-screen . . . usually, people who know they're being filmed act really stiff or silly or self-conscious. But for once in his life, Noah hadn't been self-conscious at all. Of course, he might just be a really good actor. But to be a good actor, you have to be a good liar. And Noah clearly wasn't.

"Just leave me alone, all right?" Noah said. He hopped from one foot to the other, as if he had to go to the bathroom.

"Wait." Fred held up his hands. "Come on, man." He lowered his voice and cast a quick glance around the quad, just to make sure nobody was within earshot. "You have to tell me what's going on here. If you're in trouble or something—"

"I'm not in trouble!" Noah snapped. "Now just get the hell away from me!" He tried to sidestep Fred, but he wasn't quick enough.

"Hey, I'm trying to help you," Fred whispered. He kept shifting his position so that Noah couldn't get past him, as though they were playing a game of one-on-one. "Last night, Sunday and I snuck out, and we looked in Olsen's window, and we saw this—"

"What did you see?" Noah spat. "A videotape of me and Miss Burke having sex? Do you know how ridiculous that is? I don't need your help, okay? I've got plenty of help. I'm up to my goddamn ears in help!"

Fred paused in midshuffle.

Who said anything about Miss Burke?

The hesitation was enough for Noah to spin free. Fred gaped at him as he bolted across the quad. He didn't bother following. He couldn't. His joints had frozen solid. Miss Burke? Noah was right. That *was* ridiculous.

But then, now that Fred thought about it . . . the woman in the video had the same dark hair as Miss Burke, the same lithe little body.

Jesus Christ.

It *could* have been Miss Burke, he supposed. But that scenario was pretty far off the charts, as far as believability went. No offense to Noah or anything. It was just—well, the kid wasn't exactly Calvin Klein billboard material. Still, *Noah* was the one who'd mentioned it. And he hadn't been trying to show off. Which proved two very important points: He knew about the tape, and he wasn't happy about it. Fred nodded to himself. So Miss Burke must have filmed Noah in secret. She must have set him up, the same way Burwell had set up Tony Viverito. *Man.* The people at this school . . .

"Wright!"

Well, well. Speak of the devil. Burwell was huffing toward Fred across the lawn, fists tightly clenched at his sides. Today's double-breasted suit was black with gray pinstripes. Fred shook his head. Didn't the guy have anything better to do than to spy on him? Didn't he *work*?

"Did I just see you talking to Percy?" Mr. Burwell demanded.

"Yeah," Fred said. "So?"

Burwell's face reddened. "Didn't I tell you not to associate with him?"

"I can't help it if the guy talks to me," Fred said.

"You better watch it, Wright," Burwell growled. "You're really bouncing my buttons. You've got the exhibition game against Carnegie Mansion coming up and—"

"I know, I know," Fred groaned. "What's *with* everybody and this stupid game, anyway? It's not even the regular season."

Burwell snorted. "You know, you make me sick. This isn't just any game. Carnegie Mansion is our archrival. It's the biggest game of the *year.* Parents are gonna be there. Alumni. College scouts. You gotta straighten up and fly straight. Didn't you learn anything from your friend Tony?"

"Tony? What do you mean?"

Burwell smirked. "What do you think I mean?"

It took all of Fred's self-control not to take a swing at him. That was practically a confession. It was Burwell's way of saying: *I got Tony kicked out, and there's nothing you can do about it.* The nerve of this dirtbag. Well. Maybe Fred should just forget it all. Go home. Take the year off. Get a job. That was what Burwell wanted, wasn't it? So what if Fred didn't get into Georgetown? He'd had enough—of BS (boarding school and the other kind), of crime and lies and bad laundry service and crappy cafeteria food. . . . The "prestigious" Wessex Academy. Yeah. Right. A place of honor and decency. A place where innocent kids like Tony and Noah got screwed (in Noah's case, both literally *and* figuratively), while little wieners like Winslow Ellis ran around watching porn with the headmaster and ripping people off . . .

Wait a second.

A thought had popped into Fred's brain. A slimy, low-down, despicable thought. But right now, quite honestly, he could use thoughts like these. He couldn't let Burwell win. He'd never be able to forgive himself. Besides, Sunday was counting on him. Instead of giving up, he should just start playing by their rules. Why not? In this case, he was more than justified. Burwell had said it himself: *It takes a rat to catch a rat.*

"What?" Mr. Burwell demanded. "What are you smiling about?"

Fred took a deep breath. "You know, it's a good thing I ran into you, Mr. Burwell. There's somebody I want to report to you."

He looked puzzled. "There is?"

"Yes," Fred said. "You said you wanted me to tip you off to the troublemakers. You said it didn't matter who they were. Well, this may surprise you, but the biggest troublemaker on campus is a guy you'd least suspect. His family goes back, like, a hundred years here. The dormitory where we both live is named after them."

The words didn't seem to register. Mr. Burwell simply stared at him.

"You know who I'm talking about, don't you?" Fred asked.

"I do?"

"Winslow *Ellis*," Fred said.

"Winslow Ellis," Mr. Burwell echoed. His face was blank.

"That's right." Fred shoved his hand into the front pocket of his cords and yanked out a tin of Old Hickory. "Winslow Ellis sold this to me. I wasn't going to chew it, obviously. I bought it with the sole intention of bringing it straight to you—"

"For God's sake, put that away!" Burwell hissed. He snatched the tin from Fred's grasp and shoved it into his inside jacket pocket. "What's the matter with you, Wright?" He cast a furtive glance around the quad. "You can't wave that stuff around like that. It's counterband."

"It's what?"

"Counterband," Burwell repeated.

Counterband. A new Burwellism for the list. "I see," Fred said. "Contraband. Well, I just wanted you to have it. As proof."

Burwell's face soured. "Proof of what?"

"Proof that Winslow Ellis is selling tobacco."

"How do I know you didn't buy this yourself?" Burwell asked.

Fred smiled. "Well, it would be pretty dumb of me to turn myself in, wouldn't it?"

Burwell didn't answer.

"All I'm saying is that somebody should take a look around Winslow Ellis's room," Fred said. "Now, if you're not willing to do it, I can always go to a teacher that is—"

"Don't play games with me," Burwell grunted. "I'll handle this." He glanced over both shoulders one more time, then waddled off toward the dining hall.

Fred watched him go. *Ugh.* He started to feel queasy again. Okay. That wasn't exactly the high point of his life. Part of him felt satisfied, but the other part felt . . . rodentlike. He'd never ratted out anybody before—not *ever.* Sure, Winnie had it coming to him. The little punk was due for some trouble. But to stoop so low was to bring himself down to their level.

I had to do it, though, Fred told himself. Yes. This was war. Winnie had struck first, and now he was striking back. Like he'd written to Sunday, he had to uncover the truth by any means necessary. What

63

mattered here was Noah. And if Winnie got scared enough, if his precious hide was placed in real jeopardy, then maybe he'd change. Maybe he'd come clean about the video and help Noah out of whatever kind of jam he was in.

Well, either that or Winnie would get expelled. Which wouldn't be such a tragedy, either.

"Baby, Let's Get Freaky!"
A Love Rap for Mackenzie Wilde by
Sir Mack-A-Lot, aka Hobson Crowe
(Composed during fourth-period class,
Mythology of Ancient Greece)

(Note To self: This one's a slow jam)

Sir Mack-A-Lot's here To Tell you 'bout his biz-ness
Representing New Canaan, with fat beats up in This
Rhyme I'm Throwing down, giving props To Mackenzie, yo,
That freak-a-licious Tasty young fine-looking Scorpio.
Check it out: Al Scott may have The phat money
But homegirl Mackenzie defines The word "honey."
And now it's all good, cuz I'm Through with being moody.
Yo, it's written in The stars: I'm gonna get with Mack's booty.

(Breakdown: a sample of That chick song, "What if God
Was One of Us?")

Girl, I'll give you chocolates, Take you To The prom.
You can call me Big Poppa and I'll call you Mom.
Hold up, That's wack; it sounds like I'm Oedipal.
It ain't like That, Mack; our Thing is incredible.
You got mad nectar, I got ambrosia;
You're To The word "sexy" what "end" is To "closure."
We're on The down low, making romance all sneaky,
Which is cool, but come on, baby, let's get freaky!

(Repeat breakdown.)

4

Mackenzie Wilde chewed a thumbnail as she stared at the muted, 50-inch TV screen. The enormous head of Montel Williams jabbered silently at her. His nose was easily the size of one of her hands. She held up her palm just to see. Yup. This TV was way too big for their suite. She doubted it would even fit through the door. Besides, she wanted a model with a VCR built right in. Her eyes darted across the aisle—past dozens and dozens of Montels of various sizes and hues, all gesturing in perfect unison.

"Help!" she whispered.

There were too many choices. She'd never get out of here. She really should have waited until the weekend to take a cab all the way out to the Value City Appliance Warehouse. Coming here was a major time commitment. And she definitely shouldn't have skipped Art History. Guilt had been gnawing at her ever since she'd left campus. In three full years at Wessex, going on her fourth, she was proud to say that she had skipped class just once. Aside from right now. Okay, technically she'd skipped a bunch more, but only because of stomach bugs or sniffles. Illnesses didn't count. Neither did laundry snafus. Sometimes when you sent out the laundry, it didn't come back for days—and how could you be expected to go to class when all you had to wear was a pair of leather pants and a jog bra?

Oh, right—once, her flight back from a vacation in Italy had been canceled. She'd missed two entire days that time. But that wasn't *her* fault. Her parents had foolishly booked the flight for March 27th—the most inauspicious day of that particular year, both astrologically (Mercury was in retrograde) and numerologically (27, *duh*). So of course something bad was bound to happen. She'd warned them. She was just relieved the plane hadn't crashed. And that one other time she'd *deliberately* bagged class, she'd had a very good excuse, as well.

It was sophomore year. She was on her way to third-period biology when suddenly Allison came running up to her, totally freaked because Sunday was bawling her eyes out at the Waldorf. Boyce Sutton had dumped her. Apparently, Sunday wouldn't let him go any further than second base. (Whatever that meant. For some reason, nobody had ever gone over the specifics of the base system with Mackenzie.) Anyway, Boyce had called her every name under the sun, from a "prude" to a "tease" to . . . worse. So naturally Mackenzie dropped everything. She spent the rest of the morning in the woods, reassuring Sunday that Boyce was a big, dumb loser. Anybody else would have done the same. Skipping class for friends was a righteous cause.

"That's right," she said out loud. "So I shouldn't feel guilty."

Whoops. Bad idea to keep talking to herself. There were people here. She turned back to the TVs. *Something small,* she thought. Yeah . . . small and sleek and state-of-the-art. The cost didn't matter. Mackenzie wanted to spend a lot of money. This was a peace offering, after all—a gift to bring the roommates back together, a magical salve to heal their wounds. Best of all, it was going to be a complete surprise. Her horoscope had practically demanded it: *"An act of generosity in the next few days will mend broken fences."*

So she had it all planned out. Allison and Sunday would mope back to their suite later this afternoon, feeling all tense and sour and noncommunicative . . . only to find Mackenzie sitting on the floor, watching a spanking new TV-VCR. *"Oh, my GOD!"* they'd both shriek. She'd be watching something they all loved, too. Like *Grease*. Perfect. In a matter of minutes, they'd all be hanging out together and laughing and singing "Summer Lovin'," and it wouldn't be long before the apologies and reconciliation followed. *Ta-da!*— fences mended. That was why the unit had to be just right. The last thing Mackenzie wanted to do was choose a clunky TV that didn't fit Sven Larsen's design scheme, because then Allison would get pissed.

"I can't let Allison down," she breathed.

Yeah, right. As if she hadn't let Allison down already. As if she hadn't stabbed Allison in the back. What about making out with Hobson? Mackenzie still hadn't told anyone, of course. Not even Sunday. How could she? It had been a fluke, a terrible mistake, a confluence of malevolent forces beyond her control—and yes, she'd made out with him once in the 9th grade, and yes, there was even that time she'd given herself a Tarot reading . . . no, no, no! She couldn't think about that. She was guilty enough.

She should have never gone to Hobson's room in the first place. Sure, it had been nice. Enjoyable. Thrilling, even. Especially with that music Hobson had been playing. That music was precisely what had sent her over the edge. That wicked, sexy, funky music! If only he hadn't put it on—the Earth, Fire, and Water, or whatever it was . . . it was almost like an aphrodisiac. No, it *was* an aphrodisiac. A real one. No wonder the '70s had been such a wild and promiscuous time. People couldn't control themselves. Not with music like that—

"Can I help you?"

Mackenzie turned around.

A salesgirl was standing behind her. She was about Mackenzie's age, dressed in the Value City Appliance Warehouse uniform: a cute little blue shirt and necktie combo. Her arms were folded across her chest. She had pimples.

"Well?" she asked flatly.

"Um . . ." Mackenzie squinted at her name tag. People always felt better when you called them by name. "Cecilia," she read slowly. "Hey! That's pretty. Is that really your name?"

"No," she said. "I made it up for this job."

"You *did*?"

Cecilia smiled. "Do you like what you see here, miss? Because if you don't, we have some more TVs in the back."

"No . . . I, uh—these are fine," Mackenzie answered, confused. "I was just looking."

"Oh. Just looking. I see." Cecilia didn't sound very pleased.

"What's the matter?" Mackenzie asked.

"Nothing. I'm peachy. *You're* the one who looks bummed out."

"I do?"

"Yeah. And if I had to guess, I'd say it's probably because I caught you loitering."

Mackenzie shook her head. "You what?"

"Don't play dumb with me," Cecilia snapped. "Kids like you come in here all the time, and they look and look, and they never buy anything. Sometimes they even break merchandise. Or steal it." Her voice took on a nasty bite. "Now, I'm trained to spot potential shoplifters. Most of them are just bored rich kids— spoiled brats out for a few kicks. So when I see a girl standing around and talking to herself, I get nervous. You can understand why, can't you?"

"But I—"

"If you don't want to buy anything, I suggest you leave," Cecilia said.

Mackenzie was flabbergasted. This girl actually thought she wanted to *steal* something? Mackenzie had never stolen anything in her entire life! Well, unless you counted Hobson. But no, she hadn't *stolen* Hobson; he had already broken up with Allison, and besides, Mackenzie was never going to kiss him again, not even on the cheek to say "hi" . . . and that wasn't the point. The point was that Mackenzie was a legitimate shopper. She had every right to look around for as long as she wanted—and, yes, even to talk to herself. She wasn't disturbing anyone.

"So what's it gonna be?" Cecilia asked. "Am I

gonna have to ask you to leave again, or am I gonna have to haul your ass out of here?"

Mackenzie's jaw dropped. Okay. That was it. Cecilia may have had a pretty name, but she had no right to be so rude. Now, usually, Mackenzie tried her best to avoid arguments. Especially with the New Farmington locals. (Personally, she hated how everybody at Wessex called them "townies"—as if they were all a bunch of redneck hicks. It was so elitist.) Sometimes she even apologized when she didn't have to, just for the sake of preventing a fight. But this time, she just wasn't going to stand for it. No, sirree. Not when this surprise gift was on the line. She stood on her toes and craned her neck, searching the store for a manager or—

Headmaster Olsen?

Her eyes widened.

She dove to the floor.

"What are you *doing*?" Cecilia barked.

"M-my—uh, my gum fell out of my mouth," Mackenzie stammered.

"You're not even chewing gum!"

That was true, but Mackenzie didn't respond. As cautiously as possible, she crawled to the end of the aisle and poked her head around a huge freestanding speaker. *Oh, God.* It *was* him. Even from behind, the balding scalp and wide-wale corduroy slacks were unmistakable. He was standing with some woman at a counter marked WE ALSO RENT. They were chatting with a salesman. It looked like they were returning a piece of equipment . . . yes, a video camera.

Mackenzie blinked several times. Her heart lurched. *That woman! She looks like—*

"Get outta my store!" Cecilia roared.

Mackenzie jumped back into the aisle. "Sorry," she whispered. She crouched behind a rack of TVs. "Hey, Cecilia. Will you do me a favor?" She dug into her pocket for her wallet and fished out her Visa Platinum card. "Find the smallest, most expensive TV-VCR unit you can, and ring it up." She smiled. "Oh, and it has to be black. I'll wait for you here, okay?"

Cecilia's lips tightened.

"Please?" Mackenzie begged.

Finally, with a disgusted sigh, Cecilia plucked the card from Mackenzie's fingers and vanished around the corner. "You better not try to go anywhere," she warned.

Mackenzie nodded. Her heart thumped. What if Olsen found her? Well, obviously, she'd get Sunday detention for skipping class. . . . Actually, the real question was: What was *he* doing here? And that woman. Mackenzie's stomach plummeted. It couldn't be. It didn't make any sense that *she* would be here with *him*. But Mackenzie had to be sure. She held her breath and peered around the speaker once again.

Miss Burke.

That was her, all right. Mackenzie shuddered. Miss Burke had worn that flowery dress before in class. But why would she hang out with Headmaster Olsen? She was a hip young vegetarian who read cool books and taught dance. He was an evil criminal mastermind. (True, Mackenzie had yet to determine exactly what crimes he had committed, but she knew they involved money and lying, because she'd done his star chart: Capricorn with Capricorn rising. Yikes!) The worst part was that nobody believed her. He had duped everybody—*every* single person at Wessex, except Mackenzie—into thinking that he was some kind of fool.

He must have duped Miss Burke, too.

Unless . . . no. No, it couldn't be possible.

Was Miss Burke in on it, too? Whatever *it* was?

There was only one way to find out. Somehow, Mackenzie had to get closer to them. Without being spotted. She strained her ears. She could only hear little wisps of conversation—

"MACK-in-zee Wilde!" Cecilia's voice blared from the overhead loudspeaker. She mispronounced Mackenzie's name, emphasizing the first syllable. *"MACK-in-zee Wilde, to register number four, please! We have your purchase!"*

Mackenzie's shoulders sagged. So much for trying to hide. She summoned the bravest smile she could, then dusted herself off and marched toward the counter.

"Hi, Headmaster Olsen," she sang out, waving. Maybe if she were friendly enough, he would forgive her truancy. It never hurt to brownnose every now and then.

For an instant, Headmaster Olsen looked stunned. Then he matched her phony smile. "Here comes the countess!" he replied. "Now Heaven walks on Earth!"

"Uh . . . what?" Mackenzie's eyes flashed to Miss Burke. "Hi, Miss Burke."

Miss Burke immediately stared down at her sandals.

"Twelfth Night," Headmaster Olsen said. He chuckled.

Mackenzie kept smiling politely. *Twelfth what?* Massive anxiety took hold. She had no clue what he was talking about.

"Shakespeare, Miss Wilde. Shakespeare." He sighed. "You haven't read that play?"

"Um, I don't think so. Just, you know, *Macbeth* and *King Lear.* Oh, and I saw the movie of *Midsummer Night's Dream* once." She shrugged. "Once."

He clucked his tongue. "You know, it's a shame they make films of the—"

"MACK-in-zee Wilde!"

Headmaster Olsen frowned at the ceiling. Mackenzie stole another quick peek at Miss Burke. She hadn't even said hello back. What was the matter? It wasn't like they were strangers. Mackenzie was in Miss Burke's

Twentieth-Century Literature class. She was a very active student, if she said so herself. Not only that, she often went out of her way to tell Miss Burke how much she enjoyed the class, and how she respected vegetarianism, and how she'd loved learning the hustle that night at the first Student Council meeting.

"Register four!" Cecilia bellowed. *"Now!"*

"I think they're playing your tune," Headmaster Olsen said.

"Yeah, I guess—I guess I better go," Mackenzie stammered.

"We're just returning a rented camera," Miss Burke suddenly announced. "You know, for use in the Audio-Visual Club. Sometimes we rent cameras. Instead of buying them."

Mackenzie blinked. "Oh," she said.

Miss Burke stared at her sandals again. Mackenzie waited for a follow-up remark, a greeting of some sort. None came. She turned back to Headmaster Olsen. He wasn't smiling anymore. He was glowering at Miss Burke.

"MACK-in-zee!"

"So, I'll see you back on campus," Mackenzie said quickly. "Bye-bye." She waved again, then scurried toward the front of the store. *Whoa.* Thank God she had an excuse to bolt. Talk about a weird little encounter. What was up with Miss Burke? Why had she mentioned the camera equipment? Who *cared*? Actually, Headmaster

Olsen seemed to care a lot. . . . And why hadn't Mackenzie gotten in trouble? Headmaster Olsen must have known she should be in class. He knew the ABs' schedules as well as he knew Shakespeare.

"Over here," Cecilia called impatiently, beckoning from behind a cash register.

A cardboard box sat on the counter beside Mackenzie's credit card slip. It was about fifteen inches on a side. There was an etching of a TV-VCR unit on the side facing her.

"Cool," Mackenzie said. She tried to sound as grateful as possible. "Oh, and by the way, my name is pronounced Mac-*KEN*-zie." She laughed apologetically. "I guess—"

"That'll be four hundred sixty-eight dollars and thirty-four cents," Cecilia interrupted. She held out a pen. "And I'll have to see two forms of ID for verification."

"Um . . . okay." Mackenzie peered at the box. "Wait. Is it black?"

"Black as night. Pricey, too. It's been marked up. Two forms of ID, please."

Mackenzie took the pen and absently fished for her wallet. "Thanks a lot," she said. "I really appreciate this, Cecilia." She wondered if Headmaster Olsen and Miss Burke were watching her. She was having trouble catching her breath. *Just sign for the thing and get out of here,* she commanded herself.

Her palms were moist. Her hands trembled. The wallet slipped from her grasp and fell to the counter. Cards and change spilled everywhere.

Oh, God . . . That was it. Either she was going to start laughing, or she was going to start crying. The latter seemed a lot more likely. She drew a shaky breath and smiled up at Cecilia.

"You know what's funny?" she murmured. "My horoscope said that today was supposed to be a pretty good day."

Cecilia stared at her. Then she glanced down at the jumble of cards. "I only need to see *two* forms of ID," she said.

Note Pinned to the Door of the Reed Hall Triple, 5:51 P.M.

Hey, you guys,

So I waited and waited and waited, but finally I just couldn't wait anymore. I got too hungry! I haven't eaten anything all day. My appetite's been all screwy for some reason. Okay, never mind. Anyway, I'm just running to the dining hall, and I'll be back soon. So if any of you notice anything different about the suite, well, I guess I just have to say one thing: SURPRISE!!!...

xoxo,
Mack

Note Pinned to the Door of the Reed Hall Triple, 5:57 P.M. (Previous Note Removed)

Dear Mackenzie,

While I appreciated the gesture, and while I'm sure your intentions were good, you really should have discussed the TV with me first. Sven Larsen was very specific about not having any electronic devices in the common area. You remember that, don't you? He told us that it's supposed to be a communal sanctuary, a place of quiet reflection and meditation, uncluttered by

79

distractions. Maybe you should keep it in your room. Just a thought.

I'm going to the library. I'll be back before check-in.

Allison

Note Pinned to the Door of the Reed Hall Triple, 6:22 P.M. (Previous Note Torn to Shreds)

Yo, Mack, where you aT? I been looking all over for you. So has Al. She lefT an ill noTe, yo. Too ill. I had To be all like kung fu on ThaT nonsense. BuT never mind abouT ThaT. I wanT To rap you someThing I wroTe.

you-know-who

From: Undisclosed Sender
To: pburke@wessex.edu
Subject: (no subject)
What the hell was going on at Value City?
What was that nonsense about "renting" video
equipment? I made it VERY CLEAR that if you
wanted to be a part of this, you had to keep
your mouth shut in the presence of students.
I'm not paying you to lose your composure.
You better get ahold of yourself. You're just
lucky that Mackenzie Wilde is an idiot. Don't
EVER pull that again, unless you want to lose
something a lot more valuable than fifty
thousand dollars' worth of student loan
payments. Understood?

From: pburke@wessex.edu
To: Undisclosed Sender
Subject: re: (no subject)
I'm sorry. I think I'm having second
thoughts about this whole thing. Is there
any way we can just forget about it? I don't
even really care about the money anymore.
Can't I just disappear? You can say I had a
nervous breakdown, an accident, an overdose,
whatever. You'll never hear from me again.

From: Undisclosed Sender
To: pburke@wessex.edu
Subject: re: re: (no subject)
The only way you'll disappear is if I make
you disappear. Good night, Miss Burke.

Part II
Basketball Drama of
Shakespearean Proportions

5

"Miss Burke? Can you open up, please?"

Noah pounded again on the rickety wooden door. His fist was starting to hurt. He knew she was in there; he could hear music—some kind of cheesy elevator jazz. At this point he didn't even want to confront her, or scream at her, or play out the scene he'd been rehearsing in his head all day long:

Noah: Why did you do it?

Miss Burke: I wanted you, Noah. What I want, I take.

Noah: That's a load of crap. What about the videotape?

Miss Burke: What about it? So I'm a little kinky. Some women like maids' uniforms.

Noah: But how did Winnie get his hands on it?

Miss Burke:	Hell if I know.
Noah:	So you're saying you have nothing to do with it? Or Winnie's blackmail?
Miss Burke:	Of course not. (Pulls out a sawed-off shotgun.) Now let's go get the bastard.
Noah:	Uh . . . can we have sex first?
Miss Burke:	Does a bear [bleep] in the woods? I'm naked, aren't I?

Okay, it might not happen exactly like that. But right now he didn't care. He just wanted to get out of the rain. The drizzle had started just after dinner, and now it was a full-fledged downpour. Needless to say, he hadn't had the presence of mind to don any foul-weather gear, either. He'd just slipped a tweed blazer over the T-shirt and sweatpants. Every item of clothing was completely soaked. His hair was plastered to his head. His teeth were chattering. If he stayed out here any longer, he'd probably catch pneumonia and die. Which might be a blessing.

"Miss Burke!" he screamed. "It's me, Noah! Noah Percy!"

Still nothing.

Fine. He kicked the door—hard—then took a step back and glanced up at the cozy dormitory windows. If she wanted to be a coward, no problem. He'd just fig-ure out some other way to get into her apartment. He had to act quickly, though. It was almost curfew. *Think, think, think.* . . . Well, maybe he could get to her from inside the building. Meade Hall was an old Victorian mansion, and Miss Burke's faculty apartment had originally been built as servants' quarters. (There must be some dark, ironic symbolism in that somewhere, but this was not the time to ponder it.) Generally, servants' quarters were accessible from many different parts of these old houses. He already knew of one route—through a door off the common area, at the entrance. But if she had been smart enough to lock *this* door, she probably would have locked that one, as well.

But what if there was a third door? Or even a fourth?

Yeah. There might be a hidden door in someone's room that opened on a neglected stairway or passage. That was a definite possibility. Last year, in McNeil House, Hobson had discovered a forgotten set of stairs at the back of a broom closet that led straight to the faculty apartment. (In fact, the discovery had proved to be of some archaeological significance. The stairs were littered with curious and revealing artifacts from decades past—including a broken antique hookah pipe, a tape case labeled *Foghat Rocks!* in crayon, and two tie-dyed sweatshirts, both of which smelled like diapers.) The problem was that Meade was a sophomore girls' dorm, and Noah wasn't even allowed inside without permission. . . .

Screw it.

He sloshed around the corner and burst through the main entrance.

Two girls were sitting on a couch in the common area, reading side by side. *New students.* Definitely. He'd never seen them before, and they had the unmistakable look of fresh blood: They were pale, anxious, and bony. One of them was wearing orthodontic headgear.

The door slammed shut behind him. They jerked at the sound.

"Evening, ladies," Noah said. He smiled. Rain dripped from his nose. "Do either of you have any strange doors or closets in your rooms?"

They looked at each other.

"We better get Miss Burke," Headgear whispered.

The other nodded, swallowing.

"Good idea," Noah agreed. He shook out his hair. Water splattered everywhere. Then he fell into a chair across from the couch, leaving muddy footprints in his wake.

Headgear scrambled for Miss Burke's door.

"So," Noah said to the other girl. "What are you reading?"

"I . . . uh, *Jane Eyre*," she stammered. Her eyes were wide with fear. She had braces, too.

"Good for you," Noah said. "That's a classic."

"Miss Burke!" Headgear squealed frantically. "There's a townie out here! He must have gotten onto campus somehow!"

Noah frowned. "I'm not a townie," he said. "My house is an hour away. At least."

"What do you want?" the other girl asked him. "You aren't going to hurt us, are you?"

Before Noah could think of a reply—or perhaps more importantly, examine the pitiful fact that his life had sunk to the level of terrorizing two sophomore girls—Miss Burke's door opened. It was déjà vu. She was wearing the same frayed white button-down shirt she'd been wearing the night he'd . . . well, *the night*. And she had obviously been crying again, too. Her eyes were moist. It was as if he'd traveled back in time, as if the whole sordid affair were about to happen all over again. For a second, he was worried he might pass out.

"Go to your rooms, girls," Miss Burke commanded from the doorway. Her voice was hoarse. "There's nothing to worry about. I'll handle it from here."

"Are you sure?" Headgear asked.

Miss Burke kept her gaze fixed on Noah. "I'm sure."

"Maybe you should call campus security," the second girl said.

"I already did," Miss Burke replied.

Noah laughed uneasily. "You *did*?"

Miss Burke nodded. "Go on, girls," she said. "Go upstairs."

They didn't need any more encouragement. Noah watched as they bolted from the room. *Wow.* Did he really look that bad—like some thug who'd wandered in off the streets of New Farmington? He'd never seen two people scurry up a set of stairs so fast. Their doors slammed back-to-back: *Pow! Pow!* It sounded like gunfire. He turned to Miss Burke.

"You called security?" he asked.

"Yes." She stared down at her bare feet.

"But you can't do that. I'm a respected four-year student. My dad donated the biochemistry lab."

She sniffed. "You're disturbing me, Noah," she said. The words stuck in her throat. "You're disturbing my girls. So why don't you just go away now, okay?"

Noah began to feel dizzy. In his mind's eye, he saw himself atop a mound of fecal matter in a giant toilet bowl; Miss Burke had just flushed, and the water was starting to swirl faster and faster—sucking him down into oblivion.

"See, it's just funny," he said. He was surprised he could even speak. "I mean, it's a first. Nobody's ever called security on me before. It's been a week of firsts, actually. Would you like to hear what they are?"

Miss Burke shook her head. "No," she sobbed.

"I'll take that as a yes," Noah said. "For starters, nobody's ever mistaken me for a townie before. And today was also the first time I skipped a full day of classes. Oh, and also, today was the first time I was ever blackmailed for two hundred thousand dollars. It was also the first time Winslow Ellis was ever nice to me. Let's see. What else? Oh, yeah—three nights ago was a good one. That was the first time I ever got laid—"

"Noah, please," Miss Burke choked out. "Stop it."

He opened his mouth, then hesitated. In the silence, he could hear faint strains of that annoying elevator music from her apartment. This was a useless exercise. Like choking Winnie. Clearly, Miss Burke wasn't about to confess to having a fetish for underage boys—or, conversely, tell him why she'd decided to destroy his life. He turned away. Just looking at her made him feel sick and small and ashamed. He should leave. And he should start figuring out how to get that goddamn money. This was not the time to start spouting his patented nonsense. Not with those freaking violins providing the background music.

"What are you *listening* to?" he finally demanded.

She shrugged, her hair still in her eyes. "I don't know. The radio."

"Is this the kind of music you like?"

"Yeah," she said softly. "Sometimes."

"Well, it sure isn't the Beatles," he said.

She finally looked up. Tears stained her cheeks. "What do you mean?"

"Last time I was here, you played the Beatles. Do you even *like* the Beatles? Or did Winnie just tell you that if you put on the Beatles, I'd be more likely to loosen up?"

Her eyes began to smart. "Noah, I swear to you, I—"

A loud knock cut her off. The front door opened slowly.

"Hi! Everything all right in here?"

Noah sighed. It was the captain of security himself, Biff Watson. "Planet Biff," as he was affectionately known among students. He was a sweet old man, well past retirement age and monstrously obese. He didn't bother trying to squeeze through the doorway. He stood out in the rain, a pleasant smile on his face. His sheepdog, Sparkles, sat beside him. She was panting. Her tongue hung out of her mouth. (Many years ago, Noah had formed a theory about the security force. It still held up to this day. As far as he could tell, its employees had to satisfy one of three requirements: Either they had to be [a] completely nonthreatening, [b] over seventy years old, or [c] at least three hundred pounds. As Planet Biff was the only guard who amply satisfied all three—and since he had a sheepdog named Sparkles—he was the obvious choice for captain.)

"Everything's fine, Mr. Watson," Miss Burke murmured.

"Shouldn't you be in your dorm now, young man?" Planet Biff asked Noah. "Check-in is in less than five minutes."

"Yes, sir," Noah said. "I'm sorry." He bowed his head. He *did* feel bad, at least that Planet Biff and Sparkles had had to get out of their SUV in the middle of this storm.

Planet Biff turned to Miss Burke. "Is this a disciplinary matter?" he asked.

Uh-oh. Noah held his breath. If Miss Burke said yes, then Noah would be escorted directly to Headmaster Olsen's house. And given the fact that he was on the verge of a nervous breakdown, there was a good chance he would confess everything and beg for forgiveness— in which case he would be expelled. It didn't matter how many Percys had gone to Wessex or how much money the family had donated over the years. Sex with a teacher was an offense Olsen would never forgive. It wasn't like blowing up toilets or lighting fires in the woods—or even Winnie's stock fraud, which most people found amusing, if not downright impressive. *"Gee, honey, the Wessex Academy must be a darn good school if its students are smart enough to pull a scam like that, dontcha think?"*

There was nothing smart or amusing or impressive about what Noah had done.

It didn't matter that he'd been framed, either. If the tape went public, it could tarnish the school's reputation. And that was a risk Olsen couldn't afford to take. Reputation was all that mattered to him. It was what kept the donations flowing. It was all he had. So Noah would be expelled, and then he would have to go to public school for the remainder of senior year, and he wouldn't get into any colleges, and he'd end up living under a bridge with hoboes, sniffing liquid paper and guzzling cheap cough syrup—

"Let him go," Miss Burke said. "It's nothing. A misunderstanding."

She retreated into her apartment and shut the door.

Planet Biff smiled at Noah. "A misunderstanding," he said. "Well, I suppose that's lucky for you. Come on, son. I'll give you a ride to Ellis."

Winnie was waiting in the common room when Noah arrived. He was wearing a full yellow rain suit, complete with pants and boots. He even had a matching yellow book bag.

"Jesus, dude," he said when Noah walked in. "You look terrible."

Noah smiled. "Thanks, Winnie. Thanks a lot. You look great, by the way. But, um, you know, it's almost curfew. Shouldn't you be home in Logan right now?

Planet Biff is right outside. I'm sure he could give you a ride."

Winnie shook his head. "I got permission to stay out an hour late."

"Well, have fun." Noah dashed for his door and jammed the key into the lock.

"Hey, wait up!" Winnie called. "I'm here to see *you*, dumb-ass."

The lock wouldn't turn. *Come on, come on!* Noah urged frantically. The goddamn humidity always made these old doors stick. Finally, the latch clicked and the door swung open. But by that time it was too late. Winnie was already standing beside him.

"What's your problem, dude?" Winnie asked.

Noah stepped through the door and tried to slam it in Winnie's face.

Winnie flung out an arm to stop it. "Hey, Noah—"

"You know, if I were you, I really wouldn't try to talk to me right now," Noah warned. "I'm a couple of flapjacks short of a stack. I'm pretty much capable of doing anything."

"Then this is the perfect time," Winnie said. He shoved his way past Noah and made a beeline for the desk, dripping water everywhere. "You gotta cling to that killer spirit. You gotta go for the slam dunk right after tip-off."

Again, Noah was seized by another violent fantasy

in which he saw his fist smashing Winnie's nose to bits. (Unfortunately, Winnie's nose was much smaller now, postsurgery, so it was a harder target to hit.) But Winnie *did* have an uncanny way of speaking the truth. He was right. This was it. The final round. The bottom of the ninth. Place sports cliché here. Noah had to play along with Winnie for the time being. Later, he'd have his revenge. It would be something deliciously cinematic, too. Like a piano wire around Winnie's plump neck. Or better yet, an L.L. Bean belt. And for Miss Burke? Noah would arrange for several tons of camera equipment and porn videos to fall on her head. *Splat!*

Winnie switched on Noah's computer. "Ready to make some money?" he asked.

"Sure," Noah mumbled. But he wasn't listening. He grabbed a towel from the closet to dry himself off. Something had been bothering him since lunch, and until Winnie had said the words "slam dunk," he'd been unable to pinpoint it. Or maybe he'd just been scared to admit it to himself. But somebody else was mixed up in this whole scam, too. Somebody who pretended to be Noah's friend. Somebody who had learned about his weaknesses.

Fred Wright.

Noah hurled the towel to the floor. *Yeah. More like Fred Wrong.*

Fred had to be in on the scam. There was no way he could possibly know about the tape if he wasn't involved. Did he actually expect Noah to believe that he had snuck out with Sunday in the middle of the night and seen *Olsen* watching it? Please. Noah was no Mackenzie Wilde. Sure, he may have been loopy, but he knew the difference between an imaginary conspiracy and the real deal. Olsen was a buffoonish old blowhard. He enjoyed Shakespeare, not nudity. Besides, Fred couldn't have snuck out with Sunday, because he and Sunday didn't even hang out together anymore. She'd written him off. Everybody on campus knew that. It was old news.

What Noah knew for certain was this: Fred Wrong was a guy from nowhere, a stranger, a PG—a basketball whiz who pretended to be outraged by Tony Viverito's expulsion, when all evidence seemed to indicate that *he* was the one who'd framed the kid. . . . And that was another thing. Fred was ruthless. He got rid of anybody who posed a threat. After all, Tony played the same position as Fred did. Clearly, Fred didn't care about anyone or anything but himself. Just like Winnie. They were a perfect match. Peas in a freaking pod. Maybe they were even old friends. Maybe Winnie lived a secret life—away from the Hamptons and suburban Connecticut and the Upper East Side of Manhattan—where he hatched shady plots with the likes of Fred Wrong. Anything was possible.

"Noah?"

"What?"

Winnie smiled over his shoulder. "You're not paying attention."

"Gee, I'm sorry," Noah said. "You may not know this, but I have a lot on my mind."

"Cut the crap, dude." Winnie reached into his yellow bag and yanked out a few tattered books, which he threw onto Noah's bed. "Take a look at these." He clicked the mouse to connect with the school's on-line server. "By the way, what's your password?"

"Your mother," Noah said.

"I'm being serious, butt-wad."

Noah shrugged. "Me, too." His password *was* "yourmother." But Winnie would figure that out soon enough. Noah sat on the bed and picked up the most worn of the paperbacks. It was cheaply made— all black, with plain white type. *The Criminal's Guide to Offshore Bank Accounts,* by John Doe. He had to laugh. That was funny. Hysterical, in fact. Somehow, in the past seventy-two hours, *The Noah Percy Saga, Part I,* had turned from epic masterpiece to low-budget slapstick comedy. (Soundbite: "Adam Sandler *is* Noah Percy!") And the musical track for this scene would be . . . what, exactly? Maybe "Mo' Money, Mo' Problems" by

P. Diddy. Yeah, that was an appropriate number. Noah glanced at the other two titles, *Bull Your Way Into the Market!* and *There's a Sucker Bidding Every Minute.*

Winnie busily typed away. "You weren't lying about the password," he mumbled.

"'I always tell the truth,'" Noah quoted in an Hispanic accent. "'Even when I lie.'" But as soon as he'd spoken, he regretted it. He was quoting *Scarface*, of course. It was a reflex, an old inside joke. And thinking about old inside jokes reminded Noah of the past, when he didn't have any problems. Not real ones, anyway. He tossed the book back on the bed and leaned against the pillows. Maybe he'd have an aneurysm, or spontaneously combust. Healthy people died all the time for no reason at all. Tonight might be his lucky night. He was due for a change in fortune.

"Are you reading?" Winnie asked.

"Not yet. Which of these fine volumes do you recommend first?"

"You better stop being a jerk," Winnie said. He clicked the mouse several times, jumping from Web site to Web site. "I'm trying to help you. Remember?"

"I'm sorry, I keep forgetting," Noah said. He sat up and squinted at the screen. Winnie had logged onto some financial page and was rapidly scrolling through a series of incomprehensible number and letter combinations. Were those stock quotes? Noah found himself laughing again. This was absurd. He had about the same chance of becoming an expert stock swindler in a week as he had, say, of building and piloting his own blimp.

"What's so goddamned funny?" Winnie demanded.

Noah shook his head. "Nothing. Nothing at all. But you should probably know something. The only time I ever looked at the business page of a newspaper was at Mackenzie's house, when she was training Buster to poop outside. Remember that? She only used the business section. Her theory was that all the stuff about business would somehow subconsciously seep into Buster's little doggy brain and help him with, you know, *his* 'business.' She kept on saying, 'Do your business, do your business—'"

"Bingo!" Winnie shouted.

"What?" Noah felt a twinge of dread.

Winnie spun around in Noah's chair. "I've found the perfect stock to get you going. It's an up-and-comer. It gained three-quarters of a point today, which is just right. The thing's been going up for a week now. It's already at seven and a half." He smiled. His eyes glazed over—as if he were suddenly caught in some kind of religious trance. Noah could practically see the dollar signs behind the irises. "The company's called Visi-Tech. The ticker symbol is

98

'VT.' They used to make opera glasses, but they just switched to gun sights for the military." Winnie laughed. "Thank God for defense spending."

Noah laughed, too. "Amen," he said. Then he stopped. "*Psst.* I gotta let you in on a little secret, Winnie. I have no idea what you're talking about."

Winnie grimaced. "Why do you always have to make a joke out of everything?"

"Because if I didn't, I'd be forced to think seriously about the hellish reality that is my life. And then I'd freak out and kill you. But I'm *not* joking. At least not right now."

"Whatever," Winnie muttered. He turned back to the screen. "Just start reading those books. I'll set up your homepage."

"I already have a—"

"Not your *real* homepage," Winnie snapped. "A phony one under a phony name. You're gonna be . . . let's see, something sporty, something preppy-sounding." He paused for a moment and stroked his double chin. "How about Chet Thomas? Yeah, Chet Thomas." He enunciated the name slowly. "I like the sound of that."

Noah frowned. "Don't I get to choose my own alias?"

"No," Winnie said, and he started typing again. "Now shut up and listen. Chet Thomas is everything you're not. He's a handsome Wall Street go-getter. Chicks love him. He smokes cigars and drinks scotch. And as of tonight, his homepage will be linked to all the day-trade chat rooms." Winnie's fingers flew over the keyboard as he spoke. "So. All *you* have to do is log on to these chat rooms and pump Visi-Tech. Talk about how VT is the most undervalued stock in all of human history. Use salesman lingo. A lot of capital letters and exclamation points. *Become* Chet Thomas." His voice grew feverish. "I see MASSIVE PROFITS for VT! Reliable sources from inside VT say that HUGE DEALS are in the works! So buy now! Seven and a half is DIRT CHEAP! This thing will hit FIFTY by next week, or my name isn't CHET—"

"Jesus, Winnie!" Noah cried. "I can't *do* this crap. It's me, remember? Noah Percy. The guy who couldn't convince the ticket lady at the multiplex that I was old enough to see an NC17-rated movie."

Winnie chuckled. "Aw, don't sell yourself short. You're the best BS artist at school. People are suckers, Noah. That's all you have to remember. You'll do fine."

People are suckers. Noah stared blearily at the back of Winnie's head. He couldn't argue with that one. An image of Miss Burke—in that white shirt, sipping a glass of chardonnay—flitted through his mind. He sighed. He could feel the dread again, only now it descended over him like a thick, black fog.

"Maybe you're right," Noah said. "I, of all people, should have an easy time remembering that people are suckers."

"That's the spirit," Winnie answered cheerfully. "Now, I'll spot you the first five hundred shares or so. Four thousand bucks. If you do everything I tell you, the stock'll peak at fifty in about three days. That's when you dump it. See, it's classic reverse psychology. So many people have been busted for pump-and-dump in the past few years that investors aren't *expecting* it anymore. They'll think this is the real deal, because it *is* a pump-and-dump. Get it?"

Noah nodded. Winnie could have been speaking Sanskrit. Noah hadn't understood one word—at least not past the four thousand dollars part. "Got it," he said.

"Good. You'll get about twenty-five grand, five of which will be mine. Then we move up to the big leagues."

Noah's eyes narrowed. "Wait. Didn't you just say you'd spot me *four* thousand bucks?"

"I get a one-G commission," Winnie said.

"Oh."

"Hey, if this were Wall Street, I'd keep half. Consider yourself lucky."

Noah smiled. Winnie's back was still turned to him. He could very easily grab an L.L. Bean belt from the closet and take care of the greedy fatso now. But *then* where would he be?

"I *do* consider myself lucky," he said after a moment. "Just look at me. I'm the luckiest guy on earth."

"No, you're better than lucky," Winnie said. "You're Chet Thomas."

Chet Thomas's Homepage

Hey there.

Frustrated by a sour economy? Laid off? Feeling those dot-com blues?

Don't sweat it. Because I have two questions for you.

Do you like money?

Do you like MAKING money?

If the answers are yes, then you and I have something in common.

Welcome.

BIO   *REFERENCES*   *LINKS*   *!!!!VISI-TECH!!!!*

OTHER COOL STOCK TIPS   *MY LAST VACATION TO VENICE*

WANT TO KNOW HOW TO GET CUBAN CIGARS IN THE STATES?

AN EXPERT'S GUIDE TO SINGLE MALT SCOTCH

6

What am I doing right now? Sunday wondered.

It was a rhetorical question. She knew very well what she was doing. She was trying to climb Olsen's back fence at two in the morning, in the middle of a goddamn monsoon. And she wasn't having much success. The left cuff of her sweatpants had gotten snagged on one of the fence posts, and Fred was struggling to pull her free, yanking her from under her armpits—but he kept slipping because the grass was too slick. There was no traction. Sunday had to maintain her balance by hopping up and down on her right foot. Her left leg was stuck at a ninety-degree angle. She looked like a Rockette frozen in midkick.

"Your pants are caught," Fred whispered.

"You think?" she mumbled.

He tugged at her again. The sopping wet fabric stretched a little, but that was it.

Now, Sunday had always prided herself on her ability to act rational. Or at least to *appear* rational. Where others threw fits (Allison) or turned to the occult (Mackenzie) or copped the identity of Eminem (Hobson), Sunday had always kept her sanity. Publicly, anyway. But she had to face facts: Breaking into Olsen's house, when she had been busted only forty-eight hours earlier, was not a "rational" decision. No. She was losing her mind. It was finally happening. Too many years at this freakish school—*that* was the problem. Yes, now that she'd learned that it was Miss Burke on the tape with Noah, she'd come to a grim conclusion: Wessex was an insane asylum. Seriously. There was no difference between this place and Bellevue. Or any other boarding school for that matter. They were all expensive, private institutions filled with loonies. All the ambient mental instability was bound to rub off—

"Come *on*," Fred grunted.

The elastic cuff snapped.

Sunday found herself hurtling backward. She toppled to the lawn with a messy splash, right on top of Fred—and the next instant, she was rolling around in the grass, sputtering and clawing the mud from her eyes. Her lungs heaved. Rain pelted her skin. Finally, she managed to stagger to her feet. In the darkness, she could see the tattered shred of her sweatpants bottom, hanging limply from the fencepost like a flag of surrender.

"Jesus," Fred panted. "You all right?"

"Let's just get the hell out of here," she whispered.

"What are you talking about? We made it."

She glared at him. "Made it? Fred, look at yourself. You're covered in mud right now. There's no way we can sneak into Olsen's house like this. I mean, we were so stupid. We should have thought of the weather before, you know?"

"I did," he said.

"What do you mean, you did?"

He flashed a wicked smile. "We're gonna strip," he said.

"Excuse me?"

"Check it out." He rubbed his face with a muddy sleeve and jerked a thumb toward the door that led to Olsen's kitchen. "We can leave our clothes right outside the door there and wipe ourselves clean with our shirts—you know, before we go in."

"You want to sneak in there naked," Sunday said.

Fred shrugged. "What's the difference? Nobody's gonna *see* us, right? Anyway, we're not gonna be naked. We'll be in our underwear."

"Uh, Fred, I hate to bring this up, but what if we get caught?"

He laughed. "What difference does it make what we're *wearing* if we get caught?"

"Well, I just . . ." Sunday hesitated. That was a good question, actually.

"Don't worry about it," he said. He cast a quick glance at the darkened windows on the second floor, then tiptoed toward the door.

Sunday stared at him as he began peeling off his T-shirt. *Don't worry about it.* Sure. Why worry? She was only going to strip in front of Fred—a guy with whom she had a deliberately ambiguous relationship, rife with sexual tension. No problem. On the other hand, she'd pretty much bared her soul to him in her letters. So why not bare her body, as well? *He* didn't seem to have any trouble with it. Besides, they had already slept together in the same bed. Frolicking in the seminude couldn't be far behind. Sunday lowered her eyes. Rain glistened on Fred's sinewy torso as he tugged off his sneakers and wriggled out of his pants. He was wearing a pair of oversized, striped boxer shorts. He grinned crookedly at her.

"Let's go," he whispered.

She swallowed. *It's like going swimming*, she said to herself. Right. For example, if they'd gone to the beach, and Sunday had worn a bikini, Fred would see an equal amount of flesh. It was the same exact thing. Of course it was.

She pulled off her sweatpants. Then she froze.

Well, Fred was certainly in for a treat. She'd forgotten until this very moment—but today of all days, since her laundry was low, she happened to be wearing a ludicrous American flag bra-and-panties set that Mackenzie had given to her as a joke on her sixteenth birthday. Whatever. Maybe Fred wouldn't notice. Maybe he wouldn't think it was such a big deal. Maybe *he* owned a pair of American flag boxer shorts. Her body shuddered as she pulled her sweatshirt over her head. The rain was cold. Very, very cold. Her wet hair flopped down in front of her face, dripping on the flimsy stars and stripes.

Fred wiped his hands and feet on his T-shirt. "I never knew you were such a patriot," he whispered, handing the shirt to Sunday.

Blood rushed to Sunday's face. "Yeah, well, a bunch of my ancestors fought in the Revolutionary War," she mumbled. She vainly tried to dry herself off, then dropped the T-shirt into a puddle. "Since then, all the Winthrops have worn bras and panties like this. Even the men. It's a family tradition."

"Cool," Fred said. He began chanting softly: "U–S–A . . . U–S–A . . . U–S—"

"Shhh!" She swatted his arm. For some reason, she giggled.

Fred raised a finger to his lips.

Sunday nodded. She bit her tongue. Her heart began to pound again. Fred opened the door and tiptoed into the kitchen. Sunday had to fight to keep from laughing. She really *had* gone insane. Terror was making her hysterical. She followed him as quietly as she could. The tile floor was like ice under her feet. Goosebumps rose on her arms. What were they expecting to find, anyway? A video labeled "Miss Burke Does Noah," just lying out in the open? This was so stupid. No, stupid was too generous a word. There *was* no word . . . prowling around Olsen's mansion, in dripping American flag underwear, searching for homemade porn . . . *okay, okay.* Sunday gulped. There was no point in over-thinking it. It was what it was.

Fred crept into the living room. He headed straight for the antique rolltop desk. The cover was closed. Sunday hesitated by the kitchen door as Fred crouched beside it and pulled something from his boxer shorts. Her breath came fast. She had no idea what he was doing. She squinted in the darkness at Fred's hand. There was a glint of metal. He was holding a small knife—no, a nail file. *Oh, Jesus.* She shook her head as he jammed it into the cover's keyhole. He was actually going to try to pick the lock. Another part of the plan he'd conveniently forgotten to mention. What else did he have up his sleeve? Murder?

"Fred!" she whispered.

He twisted the nail file. There was a soft *click*. The cover rolled back. He glanced over his shoulder. "What?"

Sunday blinked. "I . . ." *That* had been easy. She shrugged, then scurried up to the desk. Her eyes narrowed. There was no videotape (obviously), just a bunch of bills and letters . . . but in the dim half-light that trickled into the room from a lamp on Olsen's front lawn, she caught a glimpse of a familiar monogram: TCP. Travis and Palmer Crowe. Hobson's parents.

Phil:

You sly dog! All right, you convinced me. Put me down for twenty grand on the CM exhibition game. What's the spread—Wessex by twelve, right? Apparently, this Fred Wright kid is everything you said he is. I did a little research of my own. You don't mind, do you? I got his game tape from his old coach. You know, the tape that convinced you to admit him for a postgraduate year, despite his having the GPA of a chimp? What I'm trying to remind you of, Phil, is that I never invest blindly. That way I'm always sure of a big return. So I'm counting on your team. I don't

*need to remind you that I make a lot of
donations at this time. And why would I help
you build a new gym for a bunch of losers?*

Wessex Academy,
I sing a song of thee,
O'er hill and dale and shining sea,
My voice rings strong and free.
—Travis

Sunday stared at the note. She read it again. Then
once more. A queasy feeling gripped her stomach each
time she reached the word "chimp." She glanced at Fred.

"What's that little poem at the end?" he asked.

"That's the first verse of the school song," she
said. She tried to smile. "Have you ever heard it? It's
got a catchy melody."

Fred shook his head. "No. So, twenty grand, huh?
I guess I should feel honored." He furrowed his brow.
"Wait. How much do people usually bet on games?"

"I have no idea," Sunday mumbled. She felt sick.
"I didn't even know people did this. This whole thing
is really starting to freak me out—"

"Shh!" Fred hissed.

Sunday stiffened. "What?"

"Listen."

He pointed toward the front hall. Sunday held

her breath. She could hear something there: a series of weird, jerky squeaks—very faint, like a wet paper towel on a mirror. She leaned forward, straining her ears. Her heart thumped.

". . . and he scores!" a voice yelled.

Sunday turned to Fred.

Fred seemed puzzled. "It sounds like he's watching a game," he whispered. "Doesn't he ever sleep? I thought you said he lived like Ben Franklin."

"I thought a lot of things. What game would be on at two in the morning?" she asked. Not that she cared. But given the circumstances, it seemed an appropriate question as any.

"Maybe it's my game tape," Fred muttered. He crept toward the noise. The floorboards creaked under his bare feet.

Sunday cringed.

". . . clock is winding down. All eyes are on Phil Olsen. . . ."

Wait a second.

That was *Olsen's* voice. He was talking about himself in the third person. Sunday stared at Fred, baffled. He beckoned to her from the front hall, gesturing toward something on the other side of the arched entryway. Sunday knew the house almost as well as her own; there was a corridor there, right beside the stairwell to the second floor. It led to the cellar door.

Fred waved at her again. *"Come on!"* he mouthed silently.

But she couldn't move. Her legs were like Jell-O. This was a mistake. The same mistake, in fact, that had gotten them into this whole mess in the first place. If they had just grabbed the stationery and bolted two nights ago—the way they had *planned*—then they never would have known about the stupid sex tape at all. They would have been blissful. Happy. Ignorant. They would still be planning a silly prank on Allison. It was weird; Sunday hardly ever thought about the summer reading—but a line from *1984* summed it up best: "Ignorance is strength." Yes. Now she understood why Wessex had inspired her to read that horribly depressing book. It was a warning. A warning to stay away from the truth. The more truths you learned, the weaker you felt.

Fred beckoned once more. He disappeared around the corner.

Sunday shivered. Rain dripped from her hair and underwear. Panic was starting to take hold. She could just turn and run away. This instant. Yet even as the thought occurred to her, she stepped toward the front hall. *What is my problem?* There was some strange disconnect between her brain and her body. It was all Fred's fault. Being around him was like being on drugs. Not that Sunday knew firsthand what being on drugs was like. (Although once she'd seen Hobson's brother turn green after smoking a joint the size and shape of a carrot.) But she imagined that drugs provided the same heady, sickeningly sweet rush of terror and euphoria and awe and confusion . . . basically a jumble of emotions that made no sense.

She poked her head around the archway.

Sure enough, Fred was standing at the end of the corridor, right beside the cellar door. A sliver of light illuminated his damp, skinny body. She tried not to look at his boxer shorts.

His right hand was clamped over his mouth. He was trembling. His eyes were wide.

Sunday tiptoed toward him. Olsen's voice grew louder.

". . . you gotta love it when the season comes down to one shot," Olsen was saying. His tone was oddly melodramatic—even more so than usual—and deeper, too, as if he were imitating somebody. "This is the kind of moment Phil Olsen lives for. You can see it in his game, Marv."

Marv?

Fred pointed a shaky finger toward the light.

"This man is a living legend, Marv." Whenever Olsen spoke, his pitch descended, sort of like a piano scale in reverse. The result was that each statement ended with the same low note, which gave the last word of each sentence a peculiar emphasis. "Just look at that crossover *dribble*. Watch Olsen elude the triple-*team*. This is basketball at its *finest*."

It occurred to Sunday that she had never seen Olsen's cellar before. The dozens of times she'd been here, the door had always been closed. Interesting.

Well, no, not really. But tonight was a night of many firsts.

She peered through the doorway.

Olsen was standing at the bottom of a narrow stairwell. He had his back turned to her. He was wearing a Wessex Varsity basketball uniform. It was several sizes too small. The white tank-top jersey was emblazoned with his last name and the number 27. Love handles bulged from under it, oozing like Silly Putty over a pair of matching nylon short-shorts. She could see the outline of his tighty-whities beneath them.

"Marv, this is basketball drama of Shakespearean *proportions*," Olsen said.

As far as Sunday could tell, he was alone. Of course, she didn't have the best view from the top of the stairs. A lot of the cellar was hidden from her. Maybe Marv (*Marv?*) was on the other side of the room. She ducked down a little farther—but all she saw was a glass case lined with rows and rows of trophies. There were also a few newspaper clippings pasted to the walls. One in particular caught her eye, because the headline was printed in such a large font.

PHILLIP OLSEN INDUCTED INTO NBA HALL OF FAME

"WORLD'S SEXIEST BACHELOR" PROCLAIMS EVENT IS
GREATEST HONOR OF HIS LIFE

All at once, Olsen started moving. He pivoted to the right, then to the left. He was remarkably agile for someone so old. His love handles jiggled. His high-top sneakers screeched on the concrete floor. (So . . . *that's* where the wet-paper-towel sound had come from.) "Olsen is in fade-away *position*," he said. He raised his hands high over his head. He was holding a Nerf basketball, which he promptly tossed toward an area of the cellar just out of Sunday's line of sight. "He shoots . . . and *misses*." He scrambled away from the stairs. "But he grabs his own rebound and dunks to win the *game*. Awesome. Totally awesome. Marv, we haven't seen this kind of fire and determination since Wilt *Chamberlain*."

Fred grabbed Sunday's arm. But she was already backing away from the door. They bolted down the corridor. Their feet pattered on the floor, right over Olsen's head. Sunday's blood ran cold. She prayed for him to keep talking to "Marv." She prayed for a long-winded postgame wrap-up—a monologue of Shakespearean proportions. Fred took the lead, dashing around the corner and into the living room.

Without missing a step, he swiped the nail file from the lock—

Snap.

The nail file broke in half.

They froze.

Sunday gaped at the rolltop desk, horrified. A jagged sliver of metal protruded from the keyhole, like a tongue sticking out at her. Fred yanked it. It wouldn't budge. He turned to Sunday. His face went pale.

"Hey!" Olsen barked from the cellar. "Is anybody up there?" His voice was muffled, but the tone was threatening enough. "I'm calling campus security right now."

Fred lunged for Sunday and grabbed her hand, then sprinted to the kitchen. Sunday had no trouble keeping up with him. She'd never known she could run so fast. And as she burst back into the rain and fumbled for her waterlogged clothes, she realized she'd just experienced another first, as well. Olsen had actually *frightened* her. Now that she knew he was a certifiable madman, he was truly scary. In two short days, he'd gone from being the clownish eccentric she'd known her whole life to being another Charles Manson, a twenty-first-century Emperor Nero.

But she supposed she should look on the positive side.

If he caught them, at least he wouldn't be able to chastise her for the way she was dressed. Not unless he changed out of that basketball uniform first.

PHILLIP OLSEN INDUCTED INTO NBA HALL OF FAME

"WORLD'S SEXIEST BACHELOR" PROCLAIMS EVENT IS
GREATEST HONOR OF HIS LIFE

SPRINGFIELD, MASSACHUSETTS / AP—Forty-nine-year-old Phillip Olsen, arguably the greatest jump shooter of all time, was inducted into the NBA Hall of Fame today. The ceremony was unusual in that it honored Olsen alone—a unique occurrence in the annals of NBA history, and a testament both to his legendary status and influence on the game.

When asked for a comment before the proceedings, Olsen cryptically replied, "Words, words, words." Then he smiled at several of his girlfriends—a coterie that included Madonna, Hillary Rodham Clinton, and Julie Andrews.

According to experts, Olsen was quoting Shakespeare in order to express the futility of using mere words to describe the depth of his emotion.

Fellow Hall-of-Famer Bill Walton gave the induction speech. He described Olsen as "a man of vision, a man of heart, and a man of integrity." The two hugged for several minutes onstage after Walton presented Olsen with the certificate. Both were weeping.

"This is the greatest honor of my life," Olsen stated at the conclusion of the ceremony. Later he was asked to sink a half-court jumper, which he made on the first try.

SEE PAGE A4 FOR DETAILS

7

"Who do you think Marv is?" Sunday asked.

Fred was a little surprised by the question. Personally, he was a lot more curious about the newspaper clippings. But "Marv" was as good a place to start as any. It was better than talking about the broken nail file, at least. He and Sunday hadn't exchanged a single word in almost twenty minutes, not since sneaking back to his cramped dorm room. They hadn't bothered to put on any dry clothes. They hadn't even bothered to turn on the lights. Sunday was stretched out in her stars-and-stripes underwear on Fred's bed, staring at the ceiling. Occasionally, she shivered. Fred paced the floor in the darkness, listening to the rain. Back and forth, back and forth. The puke-green linoleum was slick with the water dripping from his boxers.

"I'm pretty sure it's Marv Albert," he said.

"Who's that?"

"He's a famous sports announcer. He was arrested about five years ago for biting a prostitute." Fred paused. "At least, I think it was a prostitute. Maybe it was just a groupie. Anyway, he was fired, but people loved him so much that all the networks hired him again."

Sunday's nose wrinkled. "Really?"

"Yup."

"So he probably wasn't down in Olsen's basement," Sunday said.

"No. See, I think Olsen was pretending to be Bill Walton. He's the guy who announces all the NBA play-off games with Marv Albert. He was this awesome basketball player in the seventies who smoked weed all the time and followed the Grateful Dead in the off-season." Fred thought for a minute. "You know, I bet that's why he talks so funny."

"Who? Olsen?"

"No. Bill Walton. All the drugs."

"Oh," Sunday said. "Wow. I never knew pro basketball was such a freak show."

"Yeah, well. Now you know why I love it so much."

"What about Walt Chamberlain? Olsen mentioned him, too."

"Wilt Chamberlain," Fred corrected. He sighed. "Yeah, he's a freak, too, I guess. Or he was. He died a few years ago. But he claimed that he had sex with twenty thousand different women while he was in the NBA. My friend Jim and I once tried to calculate exactly how many women that was per day. It came out to about eight and a half, I think."

Sunday giggled. "The half-women must have been interesting," she said.

Fred shrugged, then slumped into the metal folding chair at his desk. He knew it was his turn for a witty comeback, but he was tapped out. His thoughts were like bugs; any time one happened to scuttle through his brain, it got squashed. He wasn't sure why, either. He was used to being exhausted. Sometimes, after a really tough game or practice, when every goddamn muscle in his body was on fire, all he could do was lie down. But his mind always functioned. This mental fatigue, though . . . this was something different. Maybe it was the kind of thing that soldiers experienced after wars. Brain shutdown. Post-traumatic stress disorder. Why not? He was stressed and traumatized. His life was in disorder.

"Hey, Fred, I'm sorry about that note," Sunday murmured.

He turned to her. "What note?"

"You know, the one from Hobson's father. The

one about the gambling. It's just . . . I don't know. I can't believe the way he talked about you. Like you weren't even a *person*. Like you were a horse or something. A commodity."

Fred tried to smile. "Don't worry about it. I'm used to being treated like a piece of meat. The worse they treat you, the better you are." Mr. Otto, his old principal, had told him that once. Fred had been in the ninth grade at the time. Some jealous seniors had just beaten the crap out of him for making the varsity basketball team. He hadn't bought the line then, and he didn't buy it now. It just seemed like the right thing to say.

"I don't think you're a piece of meat," Sunday said.

"Thanks," he said. His throat tightened. He was glad it was so dark.

"I'm serious, Fred. You *can't* be a piece of meat. You're all skin and bones."

Fred tried to laugh, but the sound died somewhere in his lungs.

Sunday sat up and patted the mattress. "Come here," she breathed.

"What?"

"You need a hug," she said.

He swallowed. "I do?"

"Yes. A woman knows these things. Anyway, I need a hug, too."

"You do, huh?" Fred shook his head. She was using

that dry, flirtatious tone again—the one that made it impossible to tell whether she was being serious or not. He hated it, mostly because it frustrated him to no end. At this point, though, he honestly didn't care. He was in no condition to try to read her mind or decipher some hidden message. The truth was, he *did* need a hug. And a joke hug was better than nothing. He pushed himself out of the chair and stumbled over to the bed—straight into Sunday's open arms.

Sunday gently nuzzled against him, burying her damp hair in his neck.

"Ahh," she murmured. "That's much better."

She was right. Joke or no joke, it was pretty good. For what seemed like a very long time, the two of them sat in a cozy embrace in their rain-soaked underwear. Fred rested his chin on the top of her head. He stared at the shadowy cinder block wall. He wasn't even sure *why* it was so nice. Maybe it was because hugging Sunday provided the same sort of numb contentment that he'd experienced two nights ago, when she'd first snuck over . . . yeah, sort of like the way he felt when he closed his eyes and strapped on a pair of headphones and cranked *Axis: Bold as Love* after a really lousy day. For a couple of minutes there, he got beamed to his own magical, mellow little universe. That was it. Pure escape.

The weirdest part, though, was that under any

other circumstances (or more accurately, under the exact same circumstances, but with any other girl), he would be scheming to turn this hug into something more. He would be in scam mode. A suggestive glance here, a little murmur there. But with Sunday . . . he didn't want to ruin anything. Not that he had any idea what that "anything" was. In fact, he was more confused than ever. It was true; their relationship just seemed to get weirder and weirder with every passing moment—in a dizzying, intoxicating, impossible-to-define way. And the hug was too perfect, somehow. It was so fragile. Like a soap bubble. Any disturbance, and *pop!*—it would vanish forever.

"What are you thinking?" Sunday whispered.

"That I don't want this to end," he said.

She laughed softly. "Me, too."

Fred smiled.

"Actually, that's not true," she said. She finally pulled away and faced him. "I'm thinking that I want to kiss you."

"You what?" Fred's smile vanished. His heart thumped.

"Is that cool?"

Is that cool? "I—"

She didn't wait for him to finish his answer. He was glad. He didn't know what the hell he would have said, anyway.

*　　*　　*

The profound, life-altering, destiny-shattering, enlightening-on-a-Zen-Buddhist-scale significance of the event didn't strike Fred until the next morning.

Sunday was long gone; she'd snuck back to her dorm hours earlier, pretty much right after the little make-out session had ended. And it wasn't the make-out session itself that was so significant. (Although, it *was* significant, for many obvious reasons—not the least of which was that Fred never had to drive himself crazy about "making a move" again.) No, what had taken the night to a sublime level was one crucial realization, best summed up in five short words:

I didn't think about Diane.

It was true. Not once. Not even for an instant. He hadn't just turned a corner; he wasn't even in the same zip code anymore. He had finally freed himself from the shackles of her memory . . . from the horrible spell that her wicked, beautiful face had cast on him for so long. And the most amazing part of all was that the transformation had taken him by complete surprise. One day, he was obsessing. The next, he wasn't. And he owed it all to Sunday.

Sunday Winthrop.

A trustafarian from Greenwich. A society girl. An AB. No, he took that back. Rule number one of the Manifesto of SAFU: no abbreviations. So . . . the daughter of an alumnus. Right. The point was, who would have imagined it? Sunday Winthrop and *him*? It was crazy. It made no sense.

But then, neither did a headmaster who watched student-teacher sex tapes and announced his own late-night Nerf basketball games in the voice of Bill Walton.

Fred jumped out of bed. The rain was over. The sun was shining. He grabbed a sweatshirt and jeans from his battered dresser. To quote a time-honored cliché: He hadn't felt this good in years. True, he hadn't slept. True, if Olsen figured out who had broken the nail file in his desk, Fred would be expelled and maybe even incarcerated. But somehow, there was no fear. Only confidence. A new day was dawning! No shower necessary! Time to tear the Wessex Academy to shreds, to crucify the fiends who ran it! Olsen, Miss Burke . . . all of them. Winnie, too. None of them had any *real* power—because real power was control over a person's mind. And Fred had already conquered that enemy. The degenerates at Wessex were nothing compared to Diane. Pawns. Taking care of "The World's Sexiest Bachelor" would be gravy.

As soon as he was dressed, Fred slammed the door and headed down the spiral stairs. First stop: the Marriott. He'd have a quick dip in the woods (maybe exchange a few hostilities with Sarah Mullins—Tony Viverito's ex-girlfriend—which would be fine, because it would keep him focused on his mission), then he'd see if Mr. Burwell had spoken to Winnie yet—

"Hey, dude!"

Fred jerked to a stop. "Winnie?"

"No," Winnie said. "I'm a mirage."

If only that were true. But the fat jerk was there, all right—sprawled on the common-room couch.

"What are you doing here?" Fred asked. "It's not even nine o'clock."

Winnie grinned. "Business, dude. Business. Speaking of which, you're about due for another tin of Old Hickory, aren't you?" He unzipped his book bag.

Fred glanced at Burwell's door. "Uh . . . aren't you a little nervous about busting out the chewing tobacco right here?"

"Don't worry about it." Winnie pulled a tin from an inside pouch. "Burwell isn't around. I just saw him on the path."

"You did? Did he say anything to you?"

Winnie shrugged. "Yeah. 'Good luck kicking Carnegie Mansion's ass,' I think it was." He held out the tin and raised his thick eyebrows. "So, you want some or not?"

Fred glared at him. "He didn't say anything else?"

"No. Why would he?"

"I don't know. Burwell's always busting balls one way or another."

Winnie laughed. "Not with me, he's not." He wagged

the tin in front of his face. "Come on. Five bucks."

"All right, all right," Fred muttered. He absently shoved a hand into his pocket and fished for the money. Winnie could have meant only one thing by that annoying comeback: Burwell was looking out for him. Protecting him. Which meant that Burwell must have been in on the Noah-framing thing, too. Of course. He had to be. Why else would he let Winnie off the hook for selling tobacco? If he really wanted to end "the era of troublemaking" as he'd claimed, then Winnie already should have been packing his bags. Fred suddenly felt like puking. He'd handed Winnie to Burwell on a freaking silver platter. The "troublemaking" clearly ran deeper than Fred had previously imagined. Burwell had probably seen the tape, as well.

"So, you psyched for the big game?" Winnie asked.

Fred stared at him. "What big game?"

"The big game against Carnegie Mansion, dumbass! The game we start practicing for this afternoon." He grinned again. "The game that's gonna prove to everybody just how much of a superstar you're supposed to be."

"Oh. Yeah. Sure." Fred strode forward and shoved a crumpled bill in Winnie's hand, then snatched the tobacco and bolted out the door. He kept his head down and walked quickly. The cool morning breeze was nice. A dip would be nicer.

Correction: A dip was essential. He had to get to the Marriott *now*. He had to get away. From everyone.

It was only when he'd ducked into the woods behind the Arts Center that he realized he'd given Winnie a twenty instead of a five.

From: Undisclosed Sender
To: Undisclosed Recipient
Subject: Potential Trouble?
Something is going on between PB1 and FW. FW
asked if PB1 had "said anything" to me. He
also forgot about the game.

From: Undisclosed Sender
To: Undisclosed Recipient
Subject: re: Potential Trouble?
No kidding. Somebody broke into my house
last night. There's a broken nail file stuck
in my desk.

From: Undisclosed Sender
To: Undisclosed Recipient
Subject: re: re: Potential Trouble?
It must be PB1. He wants a copy of the tape
for himself.

From: Undisclosed Sender
To: Undisclosed Recipient
Subject: re: re: re: Potential Trouble?
And he wants influence over FW. He knows how
much we're counting on him. This game alone
will double our profit. PB1 wants a bigger
piece for himself. We'll have to take care of
him. PB2, as well. They're too risky. This is
something that's been long overdue, anyway.

Page Two of The Wessex Academy's Orientation Handbook

THE PHILOSOPHY OF THE WESSEX ACADEMY

The Wessex Academy is a college preparatory school for boys and girls, chartered by the Township Council of New Farmington, Connecticut. The School is dedicated to fostering the moral, intellectual, and physical development of its students. It challenges its students to achieve excellence and to embrace responsibility, and it expects them to act always with honor and to respect and care for others. Spiritually rooted in the principles of the Protestant faith, though nondenominational, The Wessex Academy strives to develop in its students a strong sense of moral responsibility. The administrators have always believed that the moral fortitude of the school's students gives meaning to their intellectual and physical endeavors.

THE WESSEX ACADEMY HONOR CODE

Honesty is of primary importance in an educational institution. The Wessex Academy requires its students to observe an Honor Code in all aspects of School life. Lying, cheating, and stealing are violations of the Code, and violators may be expelled. Any student who has violated the Code is expected to report his or her offense to the Headmaster or a member of the faculty. Any student who witnesses or has knowledge of a violation should ask the offender to report himself or herself as soon as possible. If the offender fails to do so, the witness is urged to report the offender to the Headmaster or a member of the faculty.

Allison Scott's teeth hurt. She'd been grinding them nonstop for the last five minutes. But she couldn't help it. She was in a state of shock.

I can't believe it's come to this.

For the first time in her life, she was alone at the Waldorf.

Could it really be true? She stood there, still as a statue in the sun-dappled clearing by the dry creek bed—her dorm-away-from-the-dorm for so many years—desperately sifting through a backlog of memories. There had to be at least one other time when she'd come here by herself. To meet someone. Like Sunday. Or Hobson. But she couldn't think of one single, solitary occasion. Not even in the eighth grade. Before she was even *enrolled* at Wessex. No, even as a thirteen-year-old, when her father had insisted that she spend a weekend on campus under the watchful tutelage of Walker Crowe and Lizzie Bryant "to become better acquainted with the social rigors of boarding school" (although Walker had been stoned the whole time, a disgrace she really should have mentioned to someone) . . . yes, even then, Allison had enjoyed the Waldorf in the snug, symbolic embrace of a group of ABs.

Not anymore.

It was horrifying. The only people who came out here by themselves were guys like Noah Percy. Weirdos. Outcasts. ABs in name only, not in substance.

But I'm not like that!

She shook her head, sniffing. Her eyes began to smart. She had to settle down. Crying was *not* behavior becoming to a Scott. No, sir. Crying was undignified. Crying was a waste of time and energy. The last time she'd burst into tears was two summers ago: on the Crowes' yacht, while they were all watching the final scene of *Titanic*. And Allison had sworn right then and there that she would never embarrass herself like that again. If Leonardo DiCaprio's death wasn't worth precious time and energy, then being stuck alone in a beautiful New England forest wasn't, either.

A fly buzzed around her head.

She swatted at it—then rubbed her eyes vigorously, inhaled, and stood straight. Her fit was over. If she were truly going to accomplish all the goals of her Seven-Part Life Plan (and she *would*, dammit) she would have to follow her own advice. Yes. She would have to use her time and energy constructively. Unlike everybody else. Unlike her friends, who seemed to have forgotten how important this semester was. It was fall of senior year. Colleges were watching. And Allison no longer had the faintest clue as to what Sunday and Mackenzie were doing with their lives. They weren't studying or participating in extracurricular activities, that was for damn sure. Not school-sanctioned ones, anyway. Mackenzie had skipped her last class yesterday to buy a TV, for God's sake.

Of course, if slacking off were the only problem, that would be fine. Nothing a little bonding couldn't cure.

But all the *secrets* . . . those were insulting. Those excluded her.

She had a few theories as to what was going on, though. Sunday was still sneaking out to spend the night with that juvenile delinquent—and lying about it, no less—while Mackenzie . . . well, Allison was pretty sure that Mackenzie was seeing somebody, too. Somebody embarrassing. She had to be. She couldn't even look Allison in the eye these days. But who? Noah, maybe? Why not? It wouldn't surprise her. Nothing could surprise her anymore. For all Allison knew,

Mackenzie was sneaking away from campus to sleep with Tony Viverito.

Eww.

It was too sordid to think about. So maybe she should stop thinking about it altogether. Why worry about her friends? They didn't seem to worry about *her.* Olsen had charged her with keeping an eye on Sunday, but on the other hand, Allison had done all she could do. If Sunday insisted on hiding the truth from her, then Allison couldn't be held responsible. If Sunday wanted to screw up her life, fine. She had Allison's blessing. So did Mackenzie. And on some level, Allison supposed she should even be happy for them. At least they were having intimate relations with members of the opposite sex. That was a lot more than *she* could say.

She sighed and slid down a tree trunk. The soil was still damp from last night's rain, but for once, she didn't even care about dirtying the seat of her Ralph Lauren pants. What was the point? She'd have a muddy butt. Big deal. It wasn't as though she had to look good for anyone. Hobson ignored her. As if he didn't even know her. As if they had never been involved. In love. Together. A couple for the ages . . .

Don't, she ordered herself. Her eyes were stinging again. *Don't—*

A twig snapped.

A couple of birds fluttered into the air. Somebody

was coming. She swallowed. Not good. She had to get a grip on herself. There was a very good chance that it was Hobson himself. Or Sunday. Or Mackenzie. And she was in no condition to deal with any of them. She took a deep breath and brushed her hair out of her eyes, then sat up straight.

Whew.

It was Winnie. Thank God for small favors.

"Hey, Allison." He peered at her curiously as he approached. "What are you doing out here all by your lonesome?"

"Waiting for Sunday." She lied automatically. "She's supposed to meet me." Her voice was hoarse. She cleared her throat and smiled. "How about you?"

He shrugged and wriggled out of his book-bag straps. "Actually, I just wanted to be by myself for a little while," he said. "You know, to clear my head before third period."

Allison bit her lip. He didn't seem embarrassed by that. Not in the least. Maybe it wasn't so weird to come out here alone. After all, Winnie was a pretty normal guy. A lot more normal than Noah, anyway. Clearing one's head was perfectly reasonable. Even noble in its own way.

"You know, I'm not really here to meet Sunday," she admitted. The words stuck in her throat. "I . . . uh, I came out here alone, too."

He hesitated. "Do you want me to leave?"

She shook her head. "No, no, of course not. Do you want *me* to leave?"

"No, that's cool." He flashed her a puzzled smile. "What's wrong?"

"Nothing," she said.

"Bull," he said. He tossed the book bag to the ground and sat on it.

Allison frowned at him. "What do you mean, bull?"

"*Something's* wrong," he said.

"How do you know?"

"Because Allison Scott doesn't come to the Waldorf by herself."

Her face reddened. "Maybe she does," she snapped. "Maybe people just don't know about it."

"Come on, Al," Winnie teased. "Everybody here knows everything about everyone else. That's what makes our lives so much fun."

"I can think of two things wrong with what you just said," she grumbled. "Two *big* things."

"What are they?"

"One: People don't know nearly as much about one another as you might think," she said. "And two: 'Fun' is hardly a word I would use to describe our lives. Or this school at all. At least, not right now."

Winnie's eyes widened in mock astonishment. "No way. Is this possible? Can Allison Scott be dissing the institution she so cherishes?"

Allison shot him a sour glance. "Make fun of me all you want, Winnie. Some of us actually care about stuff like tradition and morality and decency. But I guess that's not cool anymore. Better just to be a cynic and sell tobacco, right?"

"Hey. Play nice." Winnie's features softened a little. "All right. I'm sorry. You may not know this, Al, but I actually have a lot of respect for you."

Oh, please. Now was not the time for Winnie to start laying on the famous Ellis family BS. She probably should have told him to leave. "Sure you do," she said.

He shrugged. "It's true."

"I have a lot of respect for you, too, Winnie."

"No, really," he persisted. He leaned forward, resting his elbows on his knees, an earnest expression on his boyish face. "I think it's really incredible what you've done. I'm not kidding. You're pretty much the only person I know who has followed all the rules from the first day of freshman year. Even rules that *everyone* breaks, like dress code stuff."

She scowled. "So what?"

"So you're unique," he stated, meeting her gaze head-on. "You're not a phony. You follow the rules because you *value* the rules. Someone like me could never do that." He grinned ruefully. "Like you said, I don't have your sense of morality and decency. *Most* people here don't. That's what I'm saying. Think

138

about it, Al. There are a lot more people like me at Wessex than like you. They just take the time to hide it better. Me, I don't give a crap."

Allison stared back at him. He must be playing a joke on her. Or slapping her with some backhanded insult. Of course he was. Because in the seventeen years she'd known Winslow Ellis—yes, their whole entire lives—he'd never once taken the time to talk seriously about anything with her, much less criticize himself out loud.

"Name one rule you've broken," Winnie challenged.

"I violate the Honor Code every day," she said. "I know you sell tobacco, and I don't turn you in. How's that?"

Winnie rolled his eyes. "So. Let me get this straight. You don't go out of your way to get your friends expelled. Bravo. You're a real rebel, Al." He smiled. "Let's start over then. Say that evil rules don't count. Name one *moral* rule you've broken."

"I . . . well, I don't know." She laughed, wracking her brain. This was so stupid. "I—"

"See?" he interrupted. "I bet you never even broke the coed visitation rules when you were going out with Hobson."

Allison stopped laughing. She felt like crawling into a hole and dying. It wasn't Winnie's fault; she had the same reaction whenever Hobson's name came up. Anyway, Winnie was right. She always *had* insisted on getting permission from a dorm advisor whenever she'd visited Hobson, and vice versa. It had driven him crazy, too. Sometimes he even got mad. She'd just chalked it up to testosterone: The boy was horny, like every other teenage male at the Wessex Academy. But maybe the anger ran deeper than that. Maybe he thought she was too uptight. Maybe *that* had been the problem all along.

"I'm sorry," Winnie murmured. "I didn't mean . . ."

She lowered her gaze. "No, it's fine."

"Is that what's bumming you out?" he asked.

"Sort of," she mumbled. She kept her eyes fixed to the ground. "That and a whole lot of other stuff. Like the way my two best friends are totally unreliable."

"Sunday and Mackenzie? Why? What did they do?"

"Nothing. Everything." She moaned. "I don't know. It's just that, well, ever since school started, they've been acting like . . . like little *kids.*"

Winnie chuckled. "And this is something new? Come on. Sunday's totally repressed, and unless Jupiter aligns with Mars, Mackenzie is a basket case. Actually, if they started acting like little kids, it would be an improvement."

In spite of her dismal mood, Allison laughed again. That was pretty smart commentary, she had to admit. She lifted her head. Winnie was grinning slyly at her. Now if there was one scenario she never would have envisioned, it was this: sitting in the mud at the Waldorf, being cheered up by Winslow Ellis. But life had certainly dealt her stranger hands in the recent past. She should just appreciate it.

"Don't let them bring you down," he added.

Poor Winnie, she found herself thinking. Underneath all the scheming and baby fat, he really wasn't such a bad guy. At least he was honest with himself. That was more than most people at this school could say. Most kids at Wessex used Winnie as a measuring stick for loathsome behavior. Herself included, every so often. But Winnie was right: They were all hypocrites. Everybody else was just as loathsome.

"What?" he said. "Why are you looking at me like that? Don't try to tell me I offended you. Unless Mackenzie did your star chart or something."

"No, no." She smiled. "Nothing like that."

It was funny; now that she thought about it, Winnie wasn't even as bad-looking as people made him out to be. Sure, he was no Hobson. No amount of money would change that. But the surgery had worked wonders. No more monobrow, three fewer chins, real (meaning fake) cheekbones . . . all in all, a total makeover. Besides, blond hair and blue eyes were never a bad combo. Basketball might even help whip the rest of him into shape. Suddenly it hit her: She knew just what Winnie needed. A girlfriend. Of course! An honest-to-goodness girlfriend! Not those skeezy sluts who bought dip from him, or the sophomore townies who wanted to cash in on his trust fund . . . no, he needed somebody he could *talk* to, the way he was talking now. An AB. Like Hadley Bryant. Or Spencer Todd. Someone looking for meaningful love. Then he could drop the slimeball, tobacco-dealer act. Then he could start being real. Full-time.

"Um, Al?" he said. "Can you stop staring at me? You're really freaking me out."

She laughed. "I'm sorry. It's just—"

A series of piercing, high-pitched trills cut her off. *Bee-bee-beep. Bee-bee-beep.* They seemed to be coming from Winnie's crotch.

"What is that?" she asked.

"Nothing," he muttered. A cloud passed over his face. He shoved his hand into his pocket and yanked out a slim piece of black plastic. It wasn't until he'd flicked it open and shoved it against his ear that Allison realized what it was.

"You have a *cell phone*?" she shrieked.

"Shh." He frowned, waving his hand for her to be quiet.

Allison was stunned. She didn't know what to

think. Maybe she'd given him too much credit. Or maybe she hadn't given him enough. Cell phones weren't just prohibited at Wessex, they were . . . well, they were like sex. Everybody wanted one, and nobody was allowed to have one. Possession of a cell phone was punishable by suspension. That's how strongly the administration felt about keeping them off school grounds. They were far too much of a distraction. Which meant Winnie didn't just break the rules; he blatantly spat on them. And, in some perverse way, that was worthy of respect. They'd all seen *Scarface*, after all—

"Yeah, yeah," he said impatiently. "I know. Sal's just antsy because we're not betting against ourselves this year. Don't worry. He's just fronting us a little more than usual. I'll see you in a bit." Winnie clicked the cell phone shut and hopped to his feet, flashing an apologetic smile as he slung his book bag around his shoulders. "Sorry about that," he said. "Anyway—"

"What was that all about?" she demanded.

He shrugged innocently. "What?"

"You just got a call!" she barked. "On a cell phone!"

"I know, I know," he muttered. He shoved the phone back into his pocket. "See, Olsen put me on this special committee, and as a perk, everybody on it gets cell—"

"*What* special committee? *What* are you talking about? Who's *Sal*?"

Winnie turned and headed toward the path. "I'll tell you later," he called over his shoulder. "I need to take care of something. . . ."

"No!" she cried. She pushed herself out of the mud. "Wait!"

But it was too late. Within seconds, his footsteps faded into silence. All she heard were birds and buzzing insects. Unbelievable. She folded her arms across her chest. A sharp spasm of pain shot through her gums. Her teeth were grinding again. As well they should be. This was an outrage. Olsen had asked *her* to do his dirty work, to spy on one of her best friends—and Winnie was the one who got named to a special committee with cell phone privileges.

Was that right? Was that moral? Was that just?

No. None of the above.

But she knew what she had to do. Oh, yes. Her plan of action was suddenly crystal clear. She had to woo Sunday back from Fred at all costs. She had to turn Sunday into the model citizen that Olsen wanted her to be. *That's right.* Allison Scott would do the dirty work and more. She would crawl on her belly through a swamp if she had to. She would triumph. And at that point, *she* would be named to a special committee. And *she* would be given a cell phone. And *she* would receive many surprise calls. Right here. With Winnie. Under circumstances much like these.

Because then—and only then—would Winslow Ellis know what it felt like to be ditched at the Waldorf, wondering what the hell had happened to the Wessex tradition.

Letter from Allison to Sunday

October 9th

Dear Sun,

I have to talk to you. We're losing touch with each other. I feel so bad. This whole thing is so ridiculous. I don't even know how it began. It's senior year. We can't let a rocky start ruin a lifetime of solid friendship. Let's get together, okay? I'm ready to talk about you and Fred Wright. I have no right to judge you. And I know this is none of my business, but it doesn't make any sense for you to sleep anywhere but your own suite. Think of what your dad would say. Upholding tradition is so important to him that he went out of his way to get you his old chair, remember? (By the way, I am sorry that Sven Larsen had to get rid of the chair for aesthetic and posture-related reasons.) The point is that it would break your dad's heart to know that we aren't getting along. Just as it's breaking mine.

Sincerely,

A.

Part III
Chump City

9

"Hey! Sunday! There you are!"

Oh, God, no.

Sunday froze on the path outside Ellis Hall. Allison was supposed to be on a bus to Carnegie Mansion right now, leading her fellow students in a rousing chorus of "Wessex Academy, I Sing a Song of Thee." Sunday had deliberately hidden in Fred's room until the buses had left campus. She'd wasted a perfectly beautiful Saturday afternoon for the sole purpose of avoiding this very encounter. Well, not wasted; she'd stayed behind for a very good reason . . . but still. It didn't make sense. Allison always made a big point of appearing at so-called "events" like the Carnegie Mansion exhibition game. As the self-appointed guardian of the Wessex tradition, Allison felt it was her duty to demonstrate school spirit at appropriate moments. For last year's game, she'd even helped oversee the painting of a six-foot banner—"GO WARRIORS!"—with little hearts to dot the *i* and the exclamation point.

"I've been looking all over for you," Allison gasped, hurrying to catch up with her.

"You have? Sorry. I, um . . . I wish I'd known. I thought you were on one of the buses. You know, with everyone else."

Allison shook her head. Her forehead was damp with perspiration. She was wearing an oversized Wessex sweatshirt. For some reason, she was also clutching an expensive-looking black box with a clear plastic top. It was filled with dried flowers.

"Mackenzie and I were waiting for you," Allison said. "When you didn't show up, I decided to stay. Mackenzie went on ahead." She laughed.

"What's so funny?" Sunday asked.

"Nothing. It was just that Mackenzie said that you and I might as well stay, because she was sure that Wessex would lose by twenty-seven points. Something about Aries rising." Allison grinned. "Anyway, we can still make it. My dad's on his way to pick us up."

Sunday's smile grew strained. "Oh, jeez, Allison . . . I feel really bad. I should have told you. I *can't* go."

"You can't? Why not?"

Good question. Sunday probably should have thought of an answer before she'd opened her big mouth. Oh, well. Hopefully her face didn't look as red as it felt.

"What's wrong?" Allison asked. She cast a suspicious glance toward the dorm. "Wait a second. Does this have something to do with Fred?"

Fred! Of course. A lie suddenly snapped into place. Well done, Al. Well done.

"Yes, it does," Sunday murmured. She stared down at Allison's four-hundred-dollar Gucci loafers. "See, I can't go to the game because Fred will be there. He's gonna be playing." She swallowed, affecting a sheepish tone. "And I can't be around him right now. If you want to know, I just came from dropping off a note in his room. I had to wait until I was sure he was gone, because it . . . ah, it basically says that I can't spend any more time with him."

Allison was silent for a moment. Then she sighed.

"Oh, Sunday. I'm so sorry."

Sunday shrugged. She sniffed once. It was weird; she did feel sort of sad. But she couldn't tell if that was because she was such a good actress (meaning liar) or because Allison was so sincere about consoling her. Maybe a little of both.

"You know, it may take a while, but you'll eventually understand that this is the best decision," Allison

said softly. "It really is. For everybody concerned."
She held out the black box. "And in the meantime, I
have something that'll cheer you up."

Sunday peered at it. Her insides instantly clenched.
A brand name was printed on one side, a brand name
that she could never read without instantly slipping
into a violent rage: *sven larsen*. The lettering was in silver, all lowercase.

"What do you think?" Allison asked.

"What is it?" Sunday choked out.

"It's potpourri," Allison said. "Here." She
flipped open the cover and lifted it a little. "Smell.
It'll transport you."

A tart, fetid stench suffused Sunday's nostrils. *Jesus.*
She staggered back a few steps. The odor was stifling—
like a cross between lemon juice and a pig farm. No,
it was more like a toilet that had just been disinfected.
A dozen toilets. With industrial-strength ammonia.
Sunday had been transported, all right . . . straight to
the men's room in a seedy bus station.

"What?" Allison pouted. "You don't like it?"

"No, no." Sunday fought to breathe through her
mouth. "I'm just bummed out." The words sounded
stilted and nasal: *I'b juss bubbed out.* "Fred and all."

Allison closed the box. "You don't have to lie,"
she muttered.

"No, I'm not lying. . . ." Sunday stepped forward

and reached out for her, but Allison jerked away.

Great, now her feelings were hurt. Sunday didn't get it. What had happened to Allison this past week, anyway? One day, she was her usual controlling, bitchy, inflexible self. The next, without warning, she was an accommodating confidante. The friend she should have always been. Warm. Generous. Open. She wrote apologetic *letters*, for chrissakes. And Sunday couldn't handle it. To quote Burwell, it was a day late and an ice cube short.

"So are you coming to the game or not?" Allison asked.

"I told you, I can't," Sunday said.

Allison started grinding her teeth. "But my father will be here any minute."

"Al, I just can't, all right?" Sunday pleaded. At least she wasn't lying anymore. Sure, the excuse she gave may have been false, but she honestly had to stay. Noah's fate depended on it. The whole school's fate depended on it. And that was a matter Allison could appreciate. Or *would* appreciate, anyway—someday, after Sunday and Fred had gathered all the facts and exposed the Wessex Academy for the debased and debauched cesspool it truly was. Yes, once Allison learned the truth, she would forgive Sunday. *Then* they could start rebuilding "a lifetime of solid friendship." Or something like that.

"Sunday, listen to me," Allison stated. She tucked the box under her arm. "There's a difference between supporting your school—a school you've known and cherished since you were a toddler, I might add—and giving some random guy the wrong idea. Do you understand me?"

"I know." Sunday shrugged. She felt like pulling her hair out of her head.

"What is the matter with you, anyway?" Allison demanded. She raised her voice. The old Allison Scott was back. The flowery new facade was a little more brittle than she'd let on. "It can't just be this Fred Wright person. Something else is going on. You've been acting really, really weird recently. And I'm not the only one who's noticed."

Sunday gulped. There must be some lie she could tell, some other excuse she could make—anything to deflect the onslaught of anger. But she couldn't think of any. She was too panicked. Allison was right; she *had* been acting weird.

So she did the only possible thing she could do. She turned and ran away.

Sneaking into Olsen's mansion during the day was a lot more pleasant than it had been at night. For one thing, Sunday could actually see where she was going. She wasn't half-naked, either. It was also reassuring to know for certain that the place was empty. There wasn't the same heavy sense of inevitable, suicidal doom. And in a way, she felt almost weirdly comfortable. Of course, burglarizing Olsen had lost some of its edge. This was already the third time in less than two weeks. She was getting to be an old pro. A regular criminal.

A smile crept across her face as she tiptoed down the stairs into the cellar. It was crazy. She *should* be scared right now. Or at least anxious. Allison knew something was up. Sunday doubted that she would suspect her of doing anything like *this*, but bolting without a word hadn't been a wise move. Whatever. Allison was long gone, and that was what mattered for the time being. She and her father, and almost every single member of the faculty, as well as over half the student body . . . yes, all of them would be sitting in the Carnegie Mansion gym for the next two hours. So Sunday had plenty of time to ransack Olsen's house, find that tape of Noah and Miss Burke, and get to the bottom of this depravity once and for all.

It was a foolproof plan.

She turned on the light at the bottom of the stairwell. Her gaze slowly swept across the cellar. There didn't seem to be much down here except a big trophy case and an enormous Nerf basketball court. And the newspaper articles, of course. The sparseness of the place sort of gave her the creeps. She turned off the light and hurried back up to the first floor. But she was still smiling. She couldn't stop. *What is my problem?* she wondered.

It was another rhetorical question. The problem made her delirious. The problem was Fred Wright. Fred-Oh-So-Right . . .

Oh, brother. It was a good thing she didn't talk to herself out loud. Her mind had turned to cheese. *She* had turned to cheese. She was a walking tower of Velveeta, a florid romance novel in Donna Karan pants. And she didn't care.

She sighed, padding into Olsen's den. What amazed her most was the aura of mystery that still clung to their relationship, even *after* they'd fooled around. It was true. She still couldn't say for certain if she and Fred were an "item" or not. And that was unheard of, at least in her circle of friends. Take Boyce Sutton, for example. (*Ugh.* Looking back now, she had no clue as to why she'd found him even *remotely* attractive.) He'd asked her—formally, no less, on one knee—if he could be her boyfriend. Before they'd so much as pecked each other on the lips.

But enough reminiscing.

Now, if she were Olsen, she would keep a stash of incriminating videos . . . where? *Let me see.* Her eyes zeroed in on a familiar item: an antique wooden chest next to the TV set. She'd never taken particular notice of it before—it was just another knickknack among many—but then, she'd never had any reason to notice it. She crouched down and opened the lid.

Oh, my God.

Her face went slack.

Pay dirt. This was almost *too* easy. The chest was filled to the top with dozens of unmarked tapes. She rifled through them, her heart pounding. There was no way to tell them apart, although she supposed the Noah-and-Miss-Burke tape would be closer to the top. After a look at the cellar, it was pretty clear that Olsen didn't make much of an effort to hide his aberrant hobbies. Not within the confines of his home, anyway.

She picked one at random. Maybe she should just pop it into the VCR. She still had—

"Winthorp!"

Her head jerked toward the window. Burwell was standing on the front lawn. Today's double-breasted suit was charcoal gray.

"What are you doing here?" he barked.

Sunday hopped up and bolted from the room. She wasn't thinking. She just knew she had to get away from that face.

"Hey! Winthorp!"

Her head swam. Her chest felt tight, as if her lungs were filled with smoke.

"Come back here!" he shouted.

So. This was it. She was going to be expelled. What a pitiful way to end it all: getting caught red-handed by Burwell! Not once, but *twice*! She sprinted through the kitchen and into the backyard, hurtling over the fence with one hand while clutching the tape in the other. Trees flew past her. She supposed she should take the time to slow down and appreciate the scenic beauty of the campus. It would be her last chance, after all. Unfortunately, the instinct for survival overpowered reason. She kept running and running . . . all the way back to Ellis.

But when she reached the front porch, she realized she'd made a mistake. She should have stayed put. She could have asked Burwell the same question. What the hell was *he* doing here? If he loved Wessex so much, he shouldn't have been hanging around Olsen's front lawn. No. He should have been at Carnegie Mansion—cheering Fred Wright along with Olsen, Allison, and every other nutcase who cared about glorifying this sick, sick, sick school.

A Few Illustrative Responses to Chet Thomas's Stock Tips on Visi-Tech

From: bigtime@irc.net
To: Chet Thomas
Subject: VT is the one!
Pump-and-dump? You got to be kidding me. What's next, black-market Furbies?

From: smythe.benton.com
To: Chet Thomas
Subject: VT is the one!
We traced your ISP to the Wessex School. You kids never learn. Some other brat tried to rip us off the same way last year. Take your homepage off the net unless you want the FBI and SEC to know.

From: Grover Melnick
To: Chet Thomas
Subject: VT is the one!
Nice try, "Chet." You got your Venice vacation picture off my homepage.

From: hughes@hottix.net
To: Chet Thomas
Subject: VT is the one!
Not sure if this is the right site, but need to sell Limp Bizkit tix. Any interest in buying 20 tix for New Haven Coliseum show?

Note Slipped Under Olsen's Front Door

Dear Phil,

I know you're at the game right now. I tried to e-mail you, but the school's server is down. I'll be brief. I can't go on with this. I can't live with the shame and guilt. Keep my share of the money, please. Just let me come clean with Noah. He deserves to know the truth. Every time I see his face, part of me dies. I swear I won't jeopardize your position or our secret. I guess I just wasn't cut out for this. I was seduced by the promise of money. My family never had much. Dad was a truck driver, and Mom repaired sewing machines. We lived humbly in a ramshackle old

Well, you probably don't want to hear my life story. But I realize now that money isn't my highest priority. I'm sorry I let you down. I'm so very, very sorry.

Patricia Burke

10

A mere three minutes after tip-off, it was all very clear: The game was headed for complete catastrophe. "Warriors" was not an appropriate name for this team. "Sad Sacks" or "Rich Boys Who Suck" was more like it. Not that Fred could exclude himself from sucking. Not today. No, his personal performance was shaping up to be among the very worst of his life. He hadn't scored yet. He'd barely even touched the ball. He couldn't concentrate.

This was meant to happen, he realized.

The goddamn crowd . . . it was bigger—and louder, and more rabid, and more formally dressed—than any crowd he'd ever seen at any other high school basketball game. And he'd been to the regional conference finals last year. The freaking *regional conference finals.* A series so massive it had earned its own segment on the local news. But that was like bridge night at a retirement home compared to this. The vibe here was something along the lines of a WWF SmackDown or a monster truck rally. Yes, minus the wife-beaters and beer, it was pretty much the same faceless, frenzied mob—only with blazers and designer hair goop.

"CARNEGIE MANSION, LET'S GO!" *Clap-clap-clap.*

"CARNEGIE MANSION, LET'S GO!" *Clap-clap-clap.*

Every time they clapped, they also stamped their feet. The entire gym kept rumbling ominously, like an earthquake.

The noise wasn't to blame, though. And Fred knew it. Truth be told, he dug playing games on the road. The crowd was just a blip on his radar. So was worrying about Sunday's break-in, or knowing that Hobson's father had twenty grand riding on him, or wondering why Coach Watts hadn't organized more practices. Because usually, come game time, Fred didn't give a crap about anything. That was why he was so good. It wasn't talent. (Okay, maybe a little.) It was that he could compartmentalize distractions. Sunday could be expelled; ten thousand people could be screaming death threats; the bets on him could be in the millions—and Fred would still have scored fifteen points by the half. Easily. He could ignore it all.

Except, of course, for the one thing that had been eating away at him since he'd stepped onto the court.

Call it an Achilles heel. A quirk. Call it whatever you want. But like all ballplayers, Fred was secretly superstitious. Some guys sang opera in the shower; some guys wrote "John 3:16" in Magic Marker on their sneakers. . . . Hey, even Michael Jordan—the greatest player of all *time*—wore the same pair of underwear for every single game he ever played. So Fred wasn't alone in his odd behavior. Of course, *his* superstition was a lot subtler and less disgusting than Michael Jordan's. It was quite simple, really.

If he drank from an opposing school's water fountain before a game, he was guaranteed a stellar performance.

That was it. There was no logic involved. It was a mystical matter, one of solemn ritual and faith. But as fate would have it, the gym at Carnegie Mansion didn't *have* water fountains. At least, none that he could find. As far as Fred could tell, the place had been built by a mad scientist. It was glassy and angular and way too bright, lit up like a jailhouse on lockdown, and the showers were separate from the locker rooms, and there were no sinks (although a sink wouldn't have counted anyway), and the toilets were flushed by camera sensors—

A whistle screeched.

Fred was standing alone at one end of the court. Everybody else was standing under the opposite basket. His teammates were glaring at him. Especially Winnie.

"Wright!" Coach Watts bellowed from the sidelines. "Get your ass over here!"

Whoops. Fred jogged toward the bench.

Coach Watts's face was red and splotchy. He waved Fred into the huddle.

"Sorry, coach," Fred muttered, squeezing in between Winnie and Boyce Sutton. They were panting and stank of sweat. "I guess I kind of spaced out for a second."

"What the hell is your problem?" Coach Watts hissed. "You're a goddamn *point guard*, Wright. Do you know what that means?"

Fred shrugged.

"It means you're the quarterback! What did they teach you at public school, anyway? *You* set up the plays. Now, how can you be setting up the plays if you're halfway to Pluto?"

Boyce snickered.

"Don't laugh!" Coach Watts barked. He seized Fred's jersey, yanking Fred's face within inches of his own. "You're not on drugs right now, are you?"

"No, sir. I'm not."

He hesitated for a moment, peering into Fred's eyes. Then he let go. "What is it, then?"

"Uh . . . I'm thirsty," Fred said. "Do you know where there's a water fountain?"

Coach Watts's jaw tightened. "Thirsty. You can't play because you're thirsty." He slipped into a simpering girl's voice. "Can I have some water, please, Mommy?"

Boyce laughed again.

"Shut up, Sutton!" the coach snapped. "You want some water, Wright? Here's your water." He reached back and grabbed a bottle of Evian from the bench, then thrust it into Fred's hands. "All right, ladies," he announced. "We're going to watch the pretty baby have her drink of wa-wa. And then we're going to go back out on the court and start winning. No more screwing around. No more laziness. Do I make myself clear?"

Everybody turned to Fred.

He glanced down at the bottle.

The water was dirty. Little crumbs were floating in it.

You know what? Fred said to himself. *Screw the game.*

Screw everything, in fact. It was epiphany-time again. And in a way, this epiphany was equally as profound as the one he'd had while doing trust falls at the Marriott . . . that glorious afternoon when he'd realized that bringing people together was a lot more rewarding than using them for personal gain.

It was *good* that he was stinking up the court. It was his duty to lose right now.

True, this notion stood in furious opposition to every competitive bone in his body. But defeating Carnegie Mansion would be giving Olsen what he wanted. And that was tantamount to slapping Noah and Tony Viverito in the face. It would be slapping himself in the face, as well. After all, Olsen and Hobson's father (and who knew how many others?) were using *Fred* for personal gain—to line their pockets with cheap, greedy bets.

Yes, everything had become quite clear: There was a reason he hadn't found a water fountain. Maybe a supernatural one. Maybe not. What the hell? Maybe he was more like Mackenzie than he would like to admit. He might not believe in astrology; he owned no tarot cards or Ouija board; he didn't subscribe to the Psychic Friends Network . . . but somewhere, out there in the ether, an unseen voice was telling him: *Today, you reside in Chump City. Today, Carnegie Mansion's victory shall be your victory. TODAY, YOU LOSE.*

"Hey, Fred," Winnie said. "You gonna drink that water or what?"

He shook his head and handed the bottle back to Coach Watts. "Nope."

Coach Watts grimaced. "What do you mean, 'nope'?"

"Just what it sounds like," Fred said. A buzzer rang from the scoreboard. He turned back to the court. "Let's go. It's show time—"

Winnie clamped a hand down on his shoulder.

"Listen up, dude," he hissed into Fred's ear. "I don't know what your problem is, but you better start kicking ass if you know what's good for you."

Fred nodded, absently staring at the other players as they jogged into position. "Gotcha. I guess I'm just feeling a little woozy from all that dip I've been chewing. You owe me fifteen bucks, by the way. Or three cans of dip. Your choice."

"Shut up," Winnie growled. He waved at the bleacher section where all the Wessex faculty and alumni were sitting. "Just look at Olsen, dude. Look at his face. He's *counting* on you. Do you have any idea how much this game means to him? Or basketball in general, for that matter? Do you?"

"I'm not sure," Fred said. "I have a pretty good idea, I guess."

"Wright!" Coach Watts snapped. "Ellis! Back on the court!"

Fred wrenched free of Winnie's grip. "You heard the man," he said. He raced onto the floor. "Let's play ball."

The crowd roared.

"CARNEGIE MANSION, LET'S GO! *Clap-clap-clap.*

"CARNEGIE MANSION, LET'S GO. . . ."

Olsen *did* look pretty bummed, now that Fred noticed him. Well, either bummed or pissed. So did everybody sitting around him. Fred allowed himself a little grin. One of those guys must be Hobson's father, because they were all middle-aged and—

"Argh!" he yelped.

Time skidded to a standstill.

In that instant, there was no noise. No game, no stamping, no clapping . . . silence. The gym seemed to go black except for a single, blinding spotlight that illuminated a face three rows behind Olsen: a face as familiar to Fred as his own—a slender, pale face with thin lips, a model's nose, and green eyes. A face that had tortured him every waking moment until only a week ago. A face he hadn't seen since *January* of this year.

His blood simmered.

What the hell was Diane doing at the goddamn game, anyway? She hated basketball.

Ah, there was his answer: She was sitting next to a burly redhead, an ape who bore an uncanny resemblance to Tony Viverito. He was wearing a navy-blue nylon jogging suit. *Salvatore.* Of course. Now that they were a happy couple again, why not travel all the way to the boondocks of Connecticut to torment Diane's ex-boyfriend?

Suddenly Fred realized that Diane was staring right back at him.

She offered a tentative smile. Then she waved.

Some nerve. Some freaking nerve! He almost

laughed. Good old Diane. She really hadn't changed one bit, had she? She still had balls. Yup. It sure as hell took balls to *wave* at Fred, with Salvatore sitting right there beside her. Well, he should probably salute her in return.

He lifted his hand to give her the finger.

A basketball struck him in the left side of the head.

"Ow!"

He staggered off-balance and turned, scowling. That *hurt*. Winnie scowled back at him. Fred rubbed his temple. A Carnegie Mansion guard scooped up the ball and thundered down the court. Fred just stood there, gaping at the kid.

"Wright!" Coach Watts snarled. *"Wright!"*

But it was too late. The kid dropped in an easy lay-up, unchallenged. The gym erupted. Half the crowd jumped to their feet. People actually screamed. A new chant began to sweep through the bleachers, accompanied by the primitive *thump-thump-clap* of the song "We Will Rock You." It went: "WES-SEX SUCKS! WES-SEX SUCKS! WES-SEX SUCKS. . . ."

"What's your problem, dude?" Winnie shouted over the cacophony. "You're the point guard! Don't lift your arm if you don't want the pass!"

Fred glanced back at Diane. Her face was buried in her hands.

*　　　*　　　*

When the final buzzer rang (Wessex Warriors: 48, Carnegie Mansion Bulls: 75), the ecstatic Carnegie Mansion fans rushed the court. Fred jumped into action. He'd been benched for the entire fourth quarter, so he'd had plenty of time to figure out the fastest escape route: straight across the floor, to the right of the scorers' table, through those metal doors, then—*bam!* He would be home free, only thirty feet from the parking lot. He kept his eyes pinned to the doors as he shoved his way through the mob. Coach Watts was yelling at him, but he pretended not to hear. There wasn't much point in talking to Coach Watts right now. There wasn't much point in talking to anyone.

At the center-court line, he bumped into Diane and Salvatore.

"Fred!" Diane cried. "I'm so psyched I found you!"

His face fell. *Please, Lord, deliver me from this nightmare.* He stared down at her Birkenstocks, fighting to maintain self-control. Were those still the same pair that she'd worn back when . . . back *when*? They looked the same. But not being a Birkenstock owner himself, he didn't know what the average life expectancy was.

"Fred, this is Salvatore," Diane said. "Salvatore, this is Fred."

"I know who this prick is," Salvatore said.

Fred lifted his head, shocked. It wasn't the remark; it was that Salvatore actually spoke with the same ridiculous, offensive accent Fred had always imagined him having. *I know who diss prick iss.* It had to be an act. There was no way that voice could be real. Not unless Salvatore had spent his life trying to imitate characters from *Goodfellas* and *The Godfather*. But Diane had better judgment than that. She wouldn't date an absolute moron. Or . . . would she?

"Excuse me?" Fred asked, just to give both of them the benefit of the doubt.

Salvatore smiled. He looked like Tony's twin. "You heard me, prick."

"Okay, okay," Diane breathed, quickly stepping between them. "I thought this might—"

"*You're* calling *me* a prick," Fred interrupted. He laughed. "That's funny."

"What's so funny about it?" Salvatore asked.

Fred shrugged. "Well, *Sally*, I'm not the prick who wrote the letter to Diane talking about 'that fat old guy' from some movie who made you want to be a better man."

Diane's face turned red. "Fred, please," she whispered. "Don't—"

"No, no," Salvatore cut in. He didn't bat an eyelash. "That's fine. 'Cause, ya see, I'm not the prick who got my kid brother expelled."

Fred's stomach turned.

"That's right," Salvatore added. "Don't think I don't know about what you did."

"I—I had nothing to do with that," Fred stammered.

Salvatore sneered. He was actually a pretty big guy. Fred was taller, but Salvatore definitely had more heft. Probably a good thirty pounds more.

"I swear to God," Fred insisted.

"Nobody messes wit' da Viverito family," Salvatore said.

"Look, man, just ask anybody—"

"Maybe you didn't hear me," Salvatore interrupted again. His expression was perfectly flat, like a clothing store mannequin. "Nobody messes wit' da Viverito family," he repeated.

"I heard you," Fred said. Any feelings of guilt, fear, or remorse quickly evaporated. How was he supposed to react? *Oh, no! A Mafia-style threat from an Italian guy!* After every absurd, offensive thing he'd seen in the past few days . . . well, here was another one for the list. So. Diane's boyfriend got a kick out of exploiting his own ethnic stereotype. In order to intimidate other people. Real classy. Oh, yeah. Clearly, Fred *had* overestimated Diane's intelligence. Which was fine. Because now he knew for certain (even though he'd known for certain before) that he was truly, completely, one-hundred-percent, not-a-shred-of-doubt *over* her. She was not the idealistic hippie he'd imagined her to be. She was just a shallow phony with hippie hair. And life would be an eternal sunset cruise if he never saw her again.

"Do you understand me?" Salvatore asked.

Fred didn't answer. The conversation wasn't just pointless, it was over. Before any of them had a chance to continue it, he ran to catch up with his teammates.

Letter Slipped Under Winnie's Door

Dear Winnie,

How's it going, old buddy?

I know you're at the game right now (Go, Warriors!), but I thought I'd take this moment to give you an update on how our little pump-and-dump operation is going. I created a chart to illustrate the breakdown of returns so far. I did it just the way a real businessman or stock swindler would. It was kind of fun. Sort of like playing dress-up when you're a little girl. Whoops. I've said too much. Ignore that last part. Anyway, I got to use a calculator for the first time all year.

Chet Thomas's Visi-Tech Returns
Initial investment: $4,000.00
Number of shares: 533
Initial stock value: $7.50 per share
Current value: $2.63 per share
Net profit: - $2,598.21

So as you can see, your projections were slightly optimistic. According to you, we should have made close to $177,000.00 by now. That means you were off by $179,598.21. Now, I'm not trying to assign any blame here. You know that I respect your talents enormously. I see you as a mentor in this field: a Socrates to my Plato, a Madonna to my Britney Spears. I guess we both just underestimated the intelligence of the average cyber-investor.

Speaking of which, some of those guys were pretty mad. A lot of them, actually. I couldn't keep up with all the e-mails. Luckily, I don't have to anymore. The school's server crashed. It was too flooded.

But enough chitchat. Time is money. (You taught me that!) Okay, I know I've asked you this before—and yes, I was joking, and yes, I've borrowed $4,000.00 from you already—but do you think you can lend me $200,000.00? Because if not, I'll be expelled, and then I'll have to implicate you, and that won't be much fun for either of us. I foresee a lot of legal wrangling, bad press, court proceedings, big fines, a segment on "60 Minutes," maybe a stretch in a correctional facility. Some of this might conflict with my Christmas break plans. My family's going on safari in Zimbabwe. How about yours?

All best,
Chet Thomas aka Noah Percy

Note Slipped Under Olsen's Front Door

Interoffice memorandum

To: PO
From: PB
Date: 10/13
Re: Sunday Winthorp

I know you don't like me to contact you on paper, but I can't e-mail you. The school's Internet server crashed for some reason. We got real trouble. I saw Winthorp sneaking into your house today. I think she stole a tape. I don't know which one. She got away. What do you want me to do? I think we should kick her out. We have to take action against her and Fred Wright. They've been interfering too much. They know too much. If you don't want to kick her out, maybe we can make some kind of arrangement with her family. I know you got a relationship with them. Maybe they can give all of us something we want. They got money, and they know people out in Hollywood. So I'm just waiting for your orders. But don't misunderestimate this girl. She's a sharp cracker.

11

The mood on the bus was way too somber. It was ridiculous. Hardly anybody said a word. Mackenzie didn't understand these people at all. It wasn't like they were coming back from a *funeral*. Nobody had *died*. Besides, what did everybody expect? Losing to Carnegie Mansion was an annual tradition, like the Harvest Ball or Senior Boys' Streak Day. (Although that was a tradition she could do without this year, because she didn't relish the thought of seeing Winnie run around buck-naked.)

There was only one possible explanation. Something was going on, something in addition to an inauspicious planetary alignment. Even all the AB parents were weirdly distraught. Not *her* father, but people like Mr. Crowe. Since when did Mr. Crowe care so much about high school basketball? His son didn't even *play*. After the game, though, he could barely talk. Mackenzie had tried to say hi to him, but he just sat there with Carter Boyce's father and Hadley Bryant's father, giving Olsen mean looks and grumbling to himself. Then he'd hopped into his Porsche and sped off. He hadn't even said good-bye to his own son.

It was kind of annoying, now that she thought about it. Not the blowing-off-his-son part, although that was annoying, too. But if any of those guys had bothered to ask *her* about the game beforehand, she could have told them what would happen. It wasn't like rocket science or anything. The difference in scores should have been obvious to anybody with even the most rudimentary knowledge of numerology. CMB (Carnegie Mansion Bulls), plus WW (Wessex Warriors), plus the birth path number of the game (October 13th) equals twenty-seven. The magic number. The *evil* number. $3 + 4 + 2 + 5 + 5 + 8$. Factor in a waxing moon and Aries rising in Capricorn and bingo: You got a loss. A twenty-seven-point loss.

Duh.

But of course, nobody would ever even *think* to consult her when it came to stuff like predicting basketball scores—even though she'd been born under a Pisces moon, which meant she was blessed with natural psychic ability. (She wasn't bragging; it was just another character trait, like having brown eyes.) Nobody cared, though. Nobody except Hobson. But that didn't count, because . . . well, because she'd been trying to *avoid* him—even at big events like this one, when she didn't have to. So while he rode up front, Mackenzie sat in the rear. The whole time, she stared at the back of his blond head, chomping miserably on a piece of watermelon Bubblicious—trying not to think about how "Baby, Let's Get Freaky!" had made her blush, or how she'd spent most of the past week daydreaming about sneaking back to his room.

By the time they pulled into the campus parking lot, her mood was just as glum as everybody else's.

She blew a bubble, watching Hobson as he sauntered off toward Logan.

Pop!

Enough already. She shook her head. Today her horoscope had given her a mandate: It was time for a change. A major one. The sour energy floating around this school was starting to rub off on her, affecting the balance between her internal yin and yang. And she knew what she had to do. She had to visit Hobson one last time and officially call it quits. Today. No making out, no kissing—not even any hand-holding. Just a hug. A long one. But that was it. A clean break to free herself from the negative cycle. Hobson would understand. They couldn't keep this secret from Allison any longer. There had been too many close calls already—like his note about going "kung fu" on Allison's note. They'd been lucky Mackenzie had found that first. But if she and Hobson weren't in any danger of fooling around, there would be nothing to hide.

Right. Problem solved. Suddenly, Mackenzie felt much better. A black curtain had been lifted. Order had been restored to the cosmos. She smiled and blew another bubble, hurrying across the parking lot toward the path that led to Reed Hall. First, she would freshen up and change out of her basketball-watching clothes. She had to pick just the right outfit. Clothes made the woman. (Or was it "Clothes made the *man*"? She could never remember if that saying was gender-specific or not.) Anyway, she didn't want to give Hobson the wrong idea by wearing anything too revealing—on the other hand, she didn't want to look frumpy, either.

Sunday could help her. If Sunday was around.

Mackenzie trotted up the stairs to the third-floor triple. She still didn't understand why Sunday had blown off the game. Of course, Sunday didn't care about basketball any more than *she* did. It was strange, though—

"Hey! Stop! Hold on!"

She froze in the doorway.

What the— Sunday was around, all right. She was

179

sitting on the floor of the common area, watching something on the TV-VCR. Mackenzie's hand flew to her mouth. That was *Olsen*. Dressed like a woman. In a tiara. And really heavy makeup. And a long, old-fashioned, billowy white skirt.

"O, thou didst prophesy that time would come," he was saying. The sound was muffled. "That I should wish for thee to help me curse that bottled spider, that foul, bunch-backed toad—"

Sunday jabbed the power button.

Olsen shrank to a tiny dot in the center of the screen, then vanished.

"What is that?" Mackenzie gasped.

"Nothing," Sunday muttered hoarsely. She popped the tape from the machine, then scrambled to her feet. "Look, um, I better go—"

"Whoa, wait a second," Mackenzie interrupted. "You can't just . . ." Her voice trailed off. All of a sudden, she felt sick. Sunday's cheeks were wet. Her eyes were puffy and red. "Oh, my God, what's the matter? What's wrong, Sun?"

"Nothing." Sunday shook her head.

"Come here." Mackenzie closed the door. She walked across the room and gently took Sunday in her arms. "Tell me what's wrong, okay, sweetie?" she breathed, hugging her. "I'm sorry I barged in on you like that. What's going on?"

"I-I-I think I'm going to be expelled," she whispered shakily.

Mackenzie stepped back. "What?"

Sunday nodded, sniffling. Another tear dropped from her lashes.

"What *happened*?" Mackenzie's eyes searched her face. The gum had turned sour in her mouth. She swallowed, trying not to panic. "Tell me what's going on."

"I can't."

"You have to, sweetie. I'm not gonna let you go until you do."

Sunday held her breath for a moment. But then she seemed to give up. Her body sagged. She leaned forward, burying her face in Mackenzie's shoulder. "I would if I didn't think it would get you in trouble, too," she sobbed. "The less you know, the better. It's—it's a secret."

Mackenzie's pulse quickened. "Why? What do you mean? Can't you just give me a hint? I want to help you."

"I know, I know." Sunday drew in a deep breath and lifted her head. "Someday I'll tell you, okay?" She tried to smile, then turned away and shuffled into her room. She didn't bother closing the door. She simply flopped onto her bed, facedown. She was still holding the tape.

"How about this?" Mackenzie offered. She sat

down in the backless chair at Sunday's desk. "How about I tell you a secret, too, okay?"

Sunday curled into a fetal position. "I don't know," she said.

"You'll feel better if you talk about it. I'm not just saying that."

"Mackenzie," Sunday moaned.

"Come on."

Finally Sunday sighed. "Okay," she said. "You first."

"Me? Why me?"

"Because I want to see just how big your secret is before I tell mine," Sunday said.

Mackenzie hesitated. She started blowing a bubble. Her mind wrestled with the proposition. She knew she could trust Sunday with any secret in the world; it wasn't that . . . it was just, well, she still felt incredibly ashamed, and besides, even if she wanted to purge herself of negative energy, she didn't actually have to *confess*, although—

Pop!

She sucked the gum back into her mouth. "I fooled around with Hobson," she said.

Sunday rolled over and stared at her. *"Really?"*

Mackenzie nodded. "But it was just a one-time thing," she mumbled. "I'm not going to do it anymore."

"When did it happen?" Sunday asked.

"A couple of weeks ago." Maybe confessing wasn't such a hot idea after all. "I know it was a slimy thing to do."

"Why is it slimy? You're both single."

Mackenzie glanced at her. "Yeah, but still."

Sunday laughed softly. "You know what your problem is, Mackenzie? You're too *nice* for this school. I'm surprised you've lasted so long."

"I don't feel so nice," Mackenzie muttered.

"Take my word for it," Sunday said. She sighed and stretched out on her back, staring at the ceiling. "If *that's* your terrible secret, you deserve a gold star and a smiley face."

"You think?"

"I *know*," Sunday stated. "Take Winnie. He hangs out late-night at Olsen's and watches videos of Noah and Miss Burke having sex. How's that for a secret?"

Mackenzie blinked. "Uh . . . what?"

Sunday suddenly sat up straight. "You have to swear to God you won't tell anybody, Mack. Seriously." She gave Mackenzie a sober stare. "All right?"

"Yeah, yeah. Of course." Mackenzie nodded. She stopped chewing. The gum sat there in her mouth, like a wad of compacted garbage. The queasiness was back, spreading in diseased waves through the rest of her body. She wasn't even sure *why*. She'd only caught about half of what Sunday had said. But it was more than enough to confuse and terrify her. "Uh . . . *what* does Winnie do with Miss Burke?"

"He watches her having sex with Noah," Sunday said. "On videotape."

In spite of her horror, Mackenzie couldn't help but feel a mild pang of jealousy. "Miss Burke had sex with *Noah*?" she whispered.

"Yeah. I know. I was pretty shocked, too." Sunday shook her head. "Look, I still don't know what's going on for sure. All I know is that Miss Burke seduced Noah for some perverted reason, and when Olsen is alone he pretends to be a huge NBA star and the world's sexiest bachelor and a Shakespearean actress, and I've been breaking into his home at night and sleeping in Fred's room, and Fred broke a nail file in Olsen's desk. . . ."

Mackenzie's gum fell from her lips. It landed on her knee. She hardly noticed. Sunday kept talking—rattling off an ever-growing list of one heinous abomination after another (some, Mackenzie had already guessed, like the fact that Olsen operated a gambling ring; others, she hadn't, like the fact that Sunday actually *wore* that secondhand American flag underwear)—and the words kept coming faster and faster, so much so that Mackenzie couldn't follow them anymore. Not that she really wanted to follow them, either.

". . . and Burwell saw me stealing this tape a few hours ago," Sunday concluded.

"He *saw* you?"

Sunday nodded. "I've been hiding out here ever since. It's only a matter of time before he and Olsen come knocking at my door." A fresh batch of tears welled in her eyes. "This is it, Mackenzie. It's over. I'm gone."

"Don't say that, Sunday," Mackenzie soothed, struggling to keep the fear out of her voice. "It's not true. They can't expel you. You haven't done anything wrong."

Sunday lifted the tape. "I *stole* this, Mack. And Burwell saw me."

Mackenzie picked the gum from her knee and tossed it into the Sven Larsen waste receptacle. Then she stood. "It doesn't matter," she stated. She took a deep breath. "There's no way Olsen would ever admit to having a tape like that. It's too embarrassing. Here. Give it to me."

"Why?" Sunday asked.

"Because I'm taking it from you and putting it in a safe place." Mackenzie plucked the tape from Sunday's fingers before she could protest. "That way, on the off chance that Burwell or Olsen *do* come looking for it, they can search all they want. They can tear this place apart. And you honestly won't know where it is. You can deny even being in Olsen's house. I mean, think about it. It's your word against Burwell's. Who is Olsen gonna believe?"

Sunday blinked. A faint grin appeared on her lips.

"What?" Mackenzie asked.

"Nothing. I'm just surprised. I never knew you were so cunning."

Mackenzie shrugged. "Yeah, well, I surprise myself sometimes." She patted Sunday's head. "Don't worry about a thing."

Once again, Hobson's door was vibrating in time to the deafening beat of some rap song. The entire second floor of Logan Hall was vibrating. So were Mackenzie's bones. She didn't understand how he could listen to music so loudly. Didn't this cause some kind of skeletal damage? She could feel the rhythm in her molars, at the base of her spine.

It was kind of neat, though. Like invisible acupuncture.

BA-BOOM . . . BA-BOOM . . . BA-BOOM . . .

She took a moment to collect herself, then knocked.

Closure, she reminded herself. No listening to Earth, Fire, and Water, no talking of past lives—just in and out. *"Hobson, we can never kiss again. By the way, can you stash this tape in a safe place for me? No, I can't tell you what it is. 'Bye."* She steeled her nerves and knocked again, louder this time.

The music suddenly stopped.

"Mack? Is that you?"

"Yeah," she whispered. "How did you know—"

The door opened. Hobson was grinning. He had changed out of his jeans into a baggy, beige pants-and-sweater ensemble. It was almost like a sweat suit, only in velour. The words *Sean Jean* were stitched in script all over the fabric. A single gold chain hung around his neck. His hair was damp and freshly combed. Mackenzie couldn't keep her eyes from running down the length of his body. She'd seen plenty of Sean Jean designs before . . . just never any this, well, *sexy.* Her face was burning up. She really should have changed her own outfit.

Hobson took her hand and led her inside. "Whassup, girl?"

"Nothing, I-I . . ." She frowned. "Wait. How did you know it was me?"

"Baby, *puh-leeze."* He laughed and stretched out on the leopard skin comforter. "I saw you clockin' me at the game, yo! And on the bus, too. Just like I was clockin' you. On the DL. So I knew you'd be comin' around my way. Magnetism, yo. Magnetism."

She swallowed. Her thoughts began drifting to bad places. Namely, onto that bed. But she was too flustered and befuddled to stop staring at him. "Get it over with," she whispered to herself. It was insane: She couldn't remember *what*, exactly, she was supposed to do here. Something about leaving after a nice long hug. Hobson's effect on her short-term memory was ludicrous. Mystifying.

"Get what over with?" he asked.

"I—I don't know," she said. "It'll come to me in a sec."

He slapped the mattress. "Then have a seat, girl! You makin' me all nervous and whatnot." He cocked an eyebrow. "Yo, what's that tape you got? Sum'n freaky?"

Mackenzie slumped down on the foot of the bed. "You could say that," she mumbled.

"Yee-aah," he said with a satisfied smile. "Now that's what I'm talkin' about."

She shook her head, mustering what little clarity she could. "Hobson . . . I'm—I'm gonna have to ask you to hold on to this for me," she stammered. "And I can't tell you what it is, okay? It's just . . . it's really important."

The smile fell from his face. "What's wrong, Mack?"

"Nothing." She avoided his eyes, turning instead to a poster of Jay-Z. Her throat was dry. "I just—I can't really hang out here, okay? Not anymore."

"Whoa. Something *is* wrong." He sat up straight. "Come on. Tell me."

Her shoulders sagged. Whenever she was in

Hobson's presence, her defenses melted like ice cream under a blow-dryer. Her eyes fell to the tape. Her heart squirmed. Okay, okay . . . it wasn't really fair to ask somebody to hold on to something without revealing what that something was. No. It was cruel, in a way. Almost like torture. Anyway, she knew Hobson could keep a secret. He'd kept *them* a secret for two weeks now. Which, at this school, was definitely worth a gold star and smiley face. Any other boy would have told half the campus by now, and probably added a couple of lurid lies to beef up the story. But Hobson didn't need to brag or start rumors. He was the real deal. . . .

"Focus," she breathed.

"Focus?" he repeated, bewildered. "Mack, you gotta chill. You're buggin', yo."

She turned to him. "Listen, Hobson, you have to swear to God you won't tell anybody this," she whispered. "But something really bad is going on at this school. Miss Burke and Olsen have been taping each other doing really freaked-out stuff. See, I saw them together at Value City. They were returning a camera. A *rented* camera." Her thoughts were coming too fast; she could barely organize them. "The thing is, nobody believes me when I talk about a conspiracy. But Miss Burke filmed Olsen doing Shakespeare in drag— well, unless he filmed himself—and he filmed *her* having sex with Noah, and now Sunday's worried that—"

"Mack," Hobson whispered, delicately cutting her off. "Don't worry. I believe you."

She swallowed. "You do?"

He sighed. "I know all about it," he muttered, gazing down at his lap.

"You *do*?" she gasped.

"Well, not specifically. Not about all this." He glanced at her. "You say Olsen filmed Miss Burke having sex with Noah?"

Mackenzie nodded. Her eyes were wide. She didn't know what was more shocking—that he'd dropped the hip-hop drawl for the first time in over a year, or that he seemed totally unfazed by the question he'd just asked.

"I can't believe they did it again," he grumbled. He stared vacantly at the giant pair of turntables on the other side of the room. "They're probably hitting Noah's family up for some cash right now. *Big* cash."

"Wha-wha-what do you mean?" Mackenzie stuttered. The shift in the unseen energy here was beyond scary; she'd never felt anything like it. The aura surrounding them had grown sinister, black . . . suffocating. Like a poisonous smog.

Hobson took her hands and looked her in the eyes. "Look, Mack, I swear I won't tell anybody about

this tape, but you have to swear you won't tell anybody what I'm about to tell you. Okay?"

She nodded. She was trembling. "Of course," she
said.

"I'm serious." He flashed a little smile. "No
offense, but you don't exactly have the best reputation for keeping secrets."

"I-I-I know," she admitted. "But I promise I'll
change. For this. I'm supposed to change. It's in my
horoscope. It's meant to be."

"All right." Hobson let go of her hands. He took
a deep breath. "Remember Mr. Leonard?"

"That weird science teacher?" Mackenzie asked.
She shook her head, confused. Mr. Leonard was a
young guy—right out of college—who'd taught at
Wessex for just one year, when they were sophomores. He used to wear a fedora. That was pretty
much all that she could remember about him. Well,
that and his scraggly beard.

Hobson nodded. "Mr. Leonard sold my brother
pot. And Olsen filmed him doing it."

"What?" she cried. "Are you *serious*?"

"Very," he replied. His face was stony. "It was a
setup. Mr. Leonard acted all nice and buddy-buddy
with Walker, hanging out with him outside of class
and stuff—and the next thing Walker knew, he was
like, 'Yo, kid, you wanna score some primo buds?'

And Walker went for it. The idiot." Hobson snorted and shook his head. "He was caught on camera buying an ounce of weed for five hundred bucks. Olsen sent my parents the tape and told them that unless they wanted to see Walker get expelled, they had to send a hundred grand to some bank in the Cayman Islands."

Mackenzie gaped at him. "No way."

"Yes way," he said. "One hundred thousand dollars. That's serious paper."

"But why didn't your dad just go to the police? I mean, buying an ounce of pot is nothing compared to . . . to . . ." Her mind scrambled for the word. *"Extortion."*

Hobson laughed grimly. "You don't know my dad that well, Mack. There was no way he would involve the cops, because then the family name would get dragged through the mud. And he wasn't going to let Olsen get the best of him, either. I mean, Crowes have been coming here for, like, a hundred years. Before Olsen was even born. So he hired a private detective and found out that Olsen was placing bets with the Mafia against his own basketball team on big games. Then he made a deal—he'd give Olsen the hundred grand, as long as Olsen let him gamble, too. He earned his money back in less than three months. And Walker got to graduate."

Mackenzie didn't respond. She couldn't. It was the third or fourth time in less than an hour that she'd been confronted with a rapid-fire stream of monstrous wrongdoings—about half of which she'd missed. But one word did manage to stick. Like superglue.

"The *Mafia*?" she breathed.

He nodded. "Look, Mack, you gotta swear you won't tell anyone. And don't try to do anything. Olsen and Winnie will get what's coming to them sooner or later. But trying to mess with them is a bad idea."

"Okay. I won't tell anyone," she promised. Her stomach tied itself into a knot. Conspiracy was one thing. But this . . . *Man, oh, man.* This was bad. This went far beyond framing students. Organized crime existed in another universe entirely. The universe of *Scarface.* She had no idea what to do. Best just to stay here with Hobson. There was no way she could leave right now. Not given the state she was in. Order in the cosmos would just have to wait.

Letter Slipped Under Olsen's Door

Headmaster Olsen:

I apologize for writing you like this, but I can't contact you by e-mail right now. The school server crashed. It got overloaded with all the responses to NP's stock tips. Unfortunately, most if not all of the responses were negative. I'm really sorry. The risk factor for Phase Three was a little greater than anticipated. I honestly thought this pump-and-dump scheme would work again. Almost every book I've read on the subject says that reverse psychology works really well in the marketplace. I guess my timing was off. But it doesn't matter. We'll just send the footage to NP's father. That's probably what we should have done in the first place. Again, I'm sorry. But at least that money will cover Sal's end. Speaking of which, it's high time we get rid of FW, too. Today's game was more than an expensive mistake: it was an insult. We should take care of him when we take care of the others.

—W

Typed Note Slipped Under Winslow Ellis's Door at Logan Hall

Cute. Very cute. You're "really sorry." How touching. Well, I suppose this is my reward for trusting matters of business to a greedy, spoiled, overweight teenager. What a piece of work is man! A boy, too, it seems. But this is my fault. No matter. My most immediate concerns are not with NP. I'm sure we'll get what we want from his family. The danger lies in not getting it quickly enough. As you well know, our friend Sal was extremely displeased with the outcome of the game. His "end," as you put it, is in the six-figure range, and he's not a patient sort.

I don't have that kind of cash lying around. Nor do I have easy access to it. It's tucked away in various funds and CDs. I suggest that you make an immediate withdrawal from your personal account. NP's contribution to us—when it comes—will replenish what you spend. Think of it as a loan. The way I see matters, covering the loss is your responsibility. It's also the most sensible and expedient way to solve our little problem.

As for taking care of FW, I can think of nothing more foolish. At the very least, he and SW suspect that laws are being broken at this school, and that we're breaking them. At most, they have specific knowledge of our activities. No, our best tools in dealing with them are the same tools Sal employs when dealing with us: fear and intimidation.

The PBs are a priority. Their behavior is growing increasingly erratic. Once they're out of the picture, the mess should be easier to clean up—although we still have to concern ourselves with all the alums who placed bets. I'm sure they're thinking I swindled them and threw the game on purpose, that I lied about betting for Wessex. The spread was too big in CM's favor.

But we'll deal with one crisis at a time.

I'll handle the PBs. You handle Sal. And DON'T EVER WRITE TO ME AGAIN.

"O, from this time forth, my thoughts be bloody, or be nothing worth!" —*Hamlet*, Scene IV, Act IV

Part IV
A Small Parting Gift

12

"I think we should begin today's discussion of *The Invisible Man* with a quick look at the social climate of its time," Miss Burke announced. "The author, Ralph Ellison, captured a unique moment. . . ."

The Invisible Man. What an appropriate subject. Noah could certainly relate. Not that he'd read the book. The last book he'd read was *Bull Your Way into the Market!* He'd found it fascinating, in large part because he'd never seen so many typos and grammatical errors in a published work. But as far as assigned reading went . . . well, he hadn't glanced at a single page in quite some time. None of his teachers seemed to care, though. Least of all, Miss Burke. Which got back to the topic at hand: *He* had become the invisible man. Whenever he raised his hand, he was ignored.

Whenever he tried to speak, Miss Burke cut him off. He could have jumped up onto his desk and broken into a fervent Irish jig, and she still wouldn't have paid attention.

The sad reality was that *nobody* paid attention to him anymore.

It was true. Almost everyone seemed to go out of their way to avoid him. Students, maintenance guys . . . yes, even Planet Biff. Noah supposed he knew the reasons. He was shambling around campus these days, looking and smelling very much like a derelict—perpetually unshowered, hair bedraggled, khakis stained. He was beginning to understand how beggars felt. They, too, were invisible. He was a beggar himself. He'd begged Winnie for two hundred thousand dollars, and he still hadn't received a penny. Winnie hadn't even bothered to answer Noah's letter. (Maybe he'd tried to e-mail, but thanks to "Chet Thomas," the school's server was still down. It seemed the only place Noah *wasn't* invisible was cyberspace.) Today was the deadline, too. The two weeks were over. Time to pay up. Too bad he only had $445.31 total in his checking account.

". . . which gets back to our protagonist," Miss Burke was saying. "Any thoughts?"

Noah's hand shot up. He didn't know the answer; he hadn't even heard the question. He just wanted to torment her. This would probably be the last time he ever attended her class, so he might as well get some kicks. He glanced around the room. Almost everyone was staring at their books, pretending to be lost in deep thought. *What a bunch of fakes!* He saw them all so clearly now; he saw right through them. None of *them* had done the reading, either. Allison was grinding her teeth. No, the only person who *wasn't* putting on any kind of phony, pseudo-studious act was Mackenzie. She returned Noah's gaze, a sad smile on her face.

Sweet, sweet Mackenzie, he thought. He wondered how much she knew.

He wondered how much everybody knew.

His face darkened. The raised hand clenched into a fist. Fred Wrong sure as hell seemed to know a lot. Maybe he'd spread the word about Noah's exploits around campus. Maybe he was even charging admission to show the videotape.

But hey, why hold a grudge? Chances were that Noah would be kicked out today. Nothing could change that. (Except for two hundred thousand dollars.) But at least he'd accomplished his goal for senior year: He'd stopped obsessing over Sunday. Completely. No more daydreams about eloping with her to Ibiza. No more fantasies about accidentally walking in on her while she took a shower. Nope. The fictional relationship between them was all over.

Maybe she was through with Fred Wrong—but any girl who would stoop to be involved with him in the first place wasn't worth the mental energy. That energy could be far better spent on plotting Fred's gory demise.

"Yes? Noah? Is something wrong?"

Noah let his hand drop. Miss Burke was glaring at him.

"Wait a second," he said. "You're *talking* to me now?"

A couple of kids chuckled. Most of them, though, just kept staring at their books.

"Noah, please." She blinked a few times, swallowing. Her dark hair fell in her eyes. "Of course I'm talking to you. I'm your teacher."

"You're a little more than that," he said.

"Noah!" she cried.

"What? What difference could it possibly make? I mean, come on. Look at me. Take a whiff of my armpits. I've hit rock bottom, Miss Burke. I have nothing left to lose." He took another look around the room. Funny: Nobody was pretending to concentrate anymore. Every single pair of eyes was fixed squarely on his face. So *that's* what it took to stop being an invisible man—a threatening, inappropriate outburst. He'd have to file that one away for future reference, after he'd been disowned. "All of you guys have smelled me," he added. "Would anybody in this room classify my current odor as that of a sane person? A human being in full possession of his faculties?"

The class was dead silent.

"Don't be shy," he encouraged. "I won't be offended."

"Noah, what is your problem?" Allison barked. "Miss Burke is trying to teach, okay? Show some respect."

He twisted around and frowned at her. "Show some respect? Why? *You* don't respect Miss Burke. You think she's an idiot."

Allison's lips pressed into a tight line.

"*Psst,* Noah," Mackenzie whispered urgently. "Just mellow out, okay?"

"Why should I mellow out?" he demanded. But he wasn't directing his question at poor Mackenzie; he was directing it at Miss Burke, at Allison, at the class—at the whole goddamn school. "Why, in the name of Jeepers H. Crackers, should *I* mellow out?" His voice rose to a shout. The veins in his neck bulged. "Somebody please tell me! Because I'm dying to know! Give me one good reason!"

There was a knock on the door.

Noah slumped back into his seat, breathing hard. Miss Burke opened the door a crack.

"Yes?" she mumbled. "Is there a problem?"

"I'm sorry to interrupt. I have to see Noah Percy right away."

Noah's head jerked up. It was Olsen.

Miss Burke stepped aside. Olsen marched into the classroom. His bow tie was bright red, like the devil's. His corduroys were black. The expression on his face was stern—far sterner, in fact, than Noah had ever seen it . . . even when he'd been summoned to Olsen's office last year for blowing up a toilet.

"Come with me, Noah," Olsen commanded. "Now."

The big surprise wasn't that he'd been expelled. He'd suspected *that* the moment he'd walked into Olsen's office. No, the big surprise was that he didn't feel a thing.

This was it. The end. The tragic conclusion to *The Noah Percy Saga, Part I*. (And as everybody well knew, sequels never lived up to expectations, so *Part II* was sure to be a disappointment.) This was the moment he'd been dreading for the past two weeks, the very denouement he'd feared the most . . . yet, somehow, he couldn't conjure up any reaction at all.

He should be leaping from Olsen's couch right now. He'd been terrified of *graduating*, for God's sake. This was expulsion. There was no turning back. No cap and gown, no honors, no teacher recommendations for college, no visits as a gray-haired alumnus. He was barred from returning to campus, for all eternity—after having basically grown up here. He should be pounding his fist on Olsen's desk, demanding justice, pleading for mercy. But all he could do was sit and stare at Olsen's quivering jowls across the vast, glassy expanse of oak.

"You do understand why you're being dismissed, don't you?" Olsen asked.

"Uh . . . maybe you could just run it by me one more time," Noah said. Hopefully, hearing the explanation again would ignite some sort of latent fire inside of him. *Sheesh.* If there were ever concrete evidence that he needed therapy, this was it. He was a psychological case study in denial. Actually, this went beyond denial. He didn't even know what this was. It was a void. Pure emptiness. Maybe his emotional well had dried up in Miss Burke's classroom. What a waste! He should have saved a little of that psychosis for now.

"You had intercourse with a member of the faculty," Olsen stated. "On tape."

Noah nodded. "And?"

"And?" Olsen shouted. "And?" His face turned red. "You had sex with a teacher, Noah! And you videotaped it! Behavior like that *cannot* be tolerated at this school!"

"Yeah, yeah, I know," Noah said. "Let me just get this straight, though. Miss Burke told you that *I* videotaped it?"

Olsen threw up his hands, exasperated. "What did I just say?"

"And you believe her?"

"Of course I do," he snapped. "I've seen the tape. It's reprehensible."

Noah shook his head. "It's just . . . wow. I don't know. I'm surprised."

Olsen glared at him. "About what?"

"Have you ever known me to be a liar, Headmaster Olsen?"

"Excuse me?" His lips twisted, as if he'd just taken a bite of spoiled fruit.

"Have you ever known me to be a liar?" Noah repeated. "I mean, you've known me for most of my life. Have I ever lied to you? You know, that you can think of?"

"That's a completely inappropriate question," Olsen said.

Noah laughed. He couldn't help it. "Inappropriate? How? I've already been kicked out. *Nothing's* inappropriate. I should videotape *you* having sex, just for saying that."

Olsen's jowls wriggled. "I think you should leave, young man. You need to pack up—"

"Wait," Noah interrupted. "Excuse me. One more thing. How did you *get* the tape? I mean, who sent it to you?"

"That's none of your concern. I'm just thankful the truth surfaced. And believe me, I'll be dealing with Miss Burke in due course. You're not the only guilty party here, Noah." He shook his head and lowered his gaze. "How now, you secret black and midnight hags," he muttered somberly to himself.

Noah rolled his eyes. Perfect. What a finale. Bravo! Olsen *had* to get one last line of Shakespeare in there. He couldn't just let Noah depart on a normal, unpretentious, sane note. Then again, it wasn't the worst line he'd ever used. At least he seemed to be comparing Miss Burke to the foul, evil witches in *Macbeth*. That was pretty dead on the mark.

"Before I go, can I say something in my defense?" Noah asked.

Olsen sighed. "Fine. Although I don't much see the point."

"Thanks. I appreciate that." Noah sat up straight. "So. Allegedly, I videotaped myself having sex with Miss Burke. Now, you *do* understand what will happen to my future if this allegation gets out, and people take it seriously?" He didn't wait for Olsen to answer. "Good. I'll make this short. As the Bard says, 'Brevity is the soul of wit.' Here's the deal. Miss Burke seduced me and filmed it herself. I'm not denying I had sex with her. But I was set up. I'm being blackmailed by Winslow Ellis, Fred Wright,

206

Miss Burke, and Lord knows who else for two hundred thousand dollars. Fred actually implicated *you*, if you can believe it—"

"That's enough!" Olsen hissed. He leaned across the desk. "You never shut up, Noah. Do you realize that? You never know when to keep quiet. And I've never understood this sick compulsion you have for nonsense. Out there in the real world, people won't tolerate it. And honestly, I'm glad I'll never have to tolerate it again." He jumped to his feet and thrust a finger toward the door. "Now get out of my office, out of my school, and out of my *life*!"

Noah sat there, staring at him. Even *now*, he felt nothing. It was truly remarkable. He supposed he should consider himself lucky. Some as-yet-hidden part of his psyche was sparing him a lot of grief.

"So you're saying that you want me to leave," he said. "Gotcha." He pushed himself off of the couch. "Thanks for your time, Headmaster Olsen. Oh, one last thing, though. If you get any strange mail for somebody named Chet Thomas—a court summons, a warning from the SEC—you can go ahead and forward it to my house. He's an old friend. I have a feeling he and I are going to be pretty busy for the next couple of months."

Letter to Charles Percy from Headmaster Olsen

The Honorable Headmaster Phillip Olsen
The Wessex Academy
41 South Chapel Street
New Farmington, Connecticut 06744

Mr. Charles Percy
32 Deer Run Lane
Sherman, CT 06578

October 17

Dear Charles,

I regret to inform you that I have expelled your son, Noah. This was not a decision that I made lightly. Indeed, it is particularly vexing to me, as you and your family have faithfully supported the Wessex Academy for so many years. Sadly, I had no choice. I don't want to go into the sordid details on paper; suffice it to say that the incident involved one of our female faculty members, and that Noah's behavior was inappropriate in the extreme.

Perhaps some kind of arrangement can be made, although I'm doubtful.

Again, my most sincere regrets.

    Yours,
    The Honorable Headmaster
    Phillip Olsen

Note Taped to Fred Wright's Door

Dear Fred,

How are you? I am fine.

Let me qualify that. I <u>feel</u> fine, even though I shouldn't. You see, by the time you get this, I will be on my way to a bright future of failure and misery. That's right.

I was kicked out, Fred. And it happened in no small part thanks to you. Much appreciated, buddy!

I'm still not sure what role you played in this whole series of unfortunate events, but you played it well. You and Winnie must be proud of yourselves. I guess you'd feel more proud if I actually came through with that two hundred grand. Oh, well. I'm sorry. I just wasn't cut out for winning in the stock market. Kind of like the way you and Winnie aren't cut out for winning on the basketball court.

Oh, God. That was so lame. I'm embarrassing myself. Look what's happened to me, Fred! I've been reduced to taking cheap, sophomoric shots at you! It's beneath me! I'm smarter than that!

But enough of my yakking. Three things. One: Is public school really as bad as people say it is? Two: I left you a little something. Just a small parting gift. A token of our friendship. It's in my room. You can go right on in. It's unlocked, empty, and cleaned out. Except for what you'll find in the middle of the floor. That's for you! Go

on! Don't be afraid! Three: By all means, keep the
Guerrilla Barbershop Quartet alive. I'd suggest substituting
Hobson for me. He has a lovely singing voice. He can rap,
too. Or so he claims. He might need to brush up on his
Metallica repertoire, though.

Later, for now. (Or for the rest of our lives, I imagine.)

Your good friend,
Noah

P.S. Take care of Sunday. She was the girl of my dreams
once. I don't know what the status of your relationship is
now, but if it's good, tell her I'm very sorry I didn't lose
my virginity to her. You know, if that's not too awkward.

13

It wasn't a pile of vomit or excrement. Fred had mentally prepared himself for either possibility. It was a La-Z-Boy. Specifically, *the* La-Z-Boy. He didn't quite trust his eyes. But there it was, smack in the middle of Noah's dusty, barren room: the very same chair that Burwell had stolen from Fred at the beginning of the semester—the very same chair that had brought Noah and Fred together as friends in the first place. It was a little dirty—stained and torn in a few places—but aside from that, it was pretty much intact. Noah must have rescued it from a forgotten Dumpster somewhere.

Fred stood in the doorway. Somehow, this "parting gift" was much *worse* than human waste. It was clear that Noah had meant it as a symbolic message. Otherwise, he wouldn't have gone to the trouble of digging it out of the trash and hauling it back here. But *what* message? That he'd trusted Fred and Fred had betrayed him? That their friendship was garbage—like the chair—and had been garbage all along? That he was pissed at Fred for stealing Sunday away from him? Or was it that he just hoped Fred would get in trouble, too? It *could* be a setup. Because if Burwell found Fred in Noah's room with the forbidden La-Z-Boy, Fred would have some serious explaining to do. There was a chance *he* could be expelled.

Maybe it was all of the above.

Or maybe none. Maybe it was just one of those funny, wacky, weird, inexplicable things that Noah did for the hell of it. Like pretending to build fires or blowing up toilets. And Fred would never know the answer. That was the cruel genius of it. *You're never gonna know what this means.* In a way, it was almost like a work of art: baffling and maddening and impossible to ignore. It was Noah's final "screw you."

Wow.

Fred really had to give it to him. He deserved an award for this. No, scratch that: Burwell and Winnie and Olsen deserved the award. Yes, a round of applause was in order. They'd done it again. For the second time in three weeks, they'd managed to make Fred Wright look responsible for somebody's disgraceful expulsion.

Except this time, the "somebody" wasn't some moron's brother; it was a *friend*—Fred's only real friend at this school, in fact, aside from Sunday. Whoops. Make that former friend. Noah now hated Fred's guts, thanks to the clever hijinks of the resident villains. They *were* good. No doubt about it. After all, Noah wasn't Tony Viverito; he was shrewd. Brilliant, even. Very insightful.

And still they'd tricked him.

Come to think of it, maybe that was the reason they'd gotten rid of him: He was *too* brilliant. And he was honest. Honesty and brains were a bad combination at Wessex. If you had any modicum of intelligence, you were better off being a lying sack of feces, like Winnie. He was probably stretched out in bed right now, laughing as he counted the day's tobacco profits. Meanwhile, Noah was on a bus or train—or even worse, in a car with his parents—wallowing in shame and degradation, wondering what the hell he could do to salvage his ruined life.

But there was no point in dwelling on what Fred didn't know for certain.

What to do, what to do . . .

He figured he had two options here. One: He could continue trying to outsmart Winnie and Olsen and Burwell, sneaking around in an attempt to uncover their true motives—which, judging from all evidence to date, would be virtually impossible.

Or two: He could resort to violence.

Good. That was easy.

He stormed out of Noah's room. What time was it, anyway? About nine-thirty? Perfect. That gave him five minutes to walk over to Logan, twenty minutes to beat Winnie to a half-dead pulp, and five minutes to get home in time for check-in. Then he would lie awake while he waited for Sunday, and try not to feel guilty about the fact that he really *had* betrayed Noah—at least on some level—by waltzing into this school and hooking up with the one girl who mattered to him.

As it turned out, Fred didn't have to wait long for the last part. Sunday was running up the porch steps as he headed out the front door. She looked terrible. She was wearing sweatpants and a peacoat. Her long, dark hair was stringy. Her eyes were swollen.

"I just heard about Noah," she whispered. "Is he gone yet?"

Fred nodded.

"I can't believe this," she said. "I just . . . I can't believe it."

"Neither can I. I'll see you later." He hurried down the steps.

"Hey!" she called after him. "Where are you going?"

"To beat the crap out of Winnie. Wanna come?"

"Wait, Fred." She dashed after him. "Stop."

He shivered in the crisp night air. He probably should have worn a jacket. "But it'll feel good," he said. "I need to feel good right now."

She reached for his arm, pulling him close. "I'm pissed, too. But we can't do anything stupid right now, all right?"

"Why not? It beats doing anything smart."

"I'm *serious*," she insisted.

"I'm serious, too, Sunday," he said. "I mean, come on. What are we gonna do? Keep sneaking into Olsen's house until we get busted? We'll never find anything."

She nodded. "I know. I know."

Neither of them spoke. Crickets chirped softly all around them. The lilting drone was very peaceful. Or maybe it was just peaceful compared to Fred's own inner inferno. He had to cling to that rage. He *wanted* to do something rash, something he'd regret. It would be worth the consequences, just to see Winnie's plastic surgery ruined.

"Hey, how about we look for the tape in Olsen's office?" Sunday suggested. "We haven't looked there yet."

"When? Tonight?"

"Right now," she said.

He laughed. "Um . . . don't you think that's kind of risky?"

She shook her head. "Actually, no. Security doesn't lock the administration buildings until after check-in, anyway. Now's probably the *best* time to look. This way, we won't be breaking any rules. If we get caught, I can just say that Noah dropped something in there, and that he asked me to find it for him. You know, to send it home. Like a favorite pen or something. Or something not as lame. Some kind of weird thing that only Noah would have."

Fred stared at her. "And Olsen will go for that?" he said dubiously.

"No. He won't. But it beats getting caught in our underwear at two in the morning."

This was it. The last time. *The* very last. No more trespassing. No more poking around in places they shouldn't. Before they opened Olsen's office door, Fred made Sunday swear that from this moment forward, she would only sneak out to go to Fred's room. Period.

"Okay, okay," Sunday whispered impatiently. "I swear."

"You have to mean it," he said. "Think of it as the first amendment to the Manifesto."

"I mean it." She glanced in either direction down the long, dark, marble hallway. "Now come on. We only have, like, ten minutes."

Fred pushed the door open. He knew she didn't mean it. Neither did he, really. Normally, she was the cautious one, though. The role-reversal was kind of funny. Well, not *funny*. Nothing was really funny anymore.

"You didn't bring a nail file again, did you?" she asked, scooting around to the other side of Olsen's enormous desk.

"Nope," he mumbled. "You saw how well it worked the last time." He closed the door behind him and glanced around. Remarkably, he'd never actually set foot inside here. *Jeez.* Compared to Principal Otto's office at Lincoln, this place was a freaking palace. The Oriental rug, the grandfather clock, the leather couch, the book-lined shelves . . . the bust of Shakespeare over the mantle probably cost as much as Otto's entire furniture set. Fred sneered. *Money, money, money.* He could smell its stink. It was like invisible slime, dripping from every surface. The display wasn't just excessive; it was foul. Being rich was one thing. Flaunting your wealth when you were criminally insane was something else.

"Hey, Fred," Sunday breathed. "Check this out."

The desk drawer was unlocked. Sunday had yanked it open and was rifling through a bunch of papers.

She paused, then pulled one out and squinted at it. She shook her head.

"What?" Fred whispered. He tiptoed to her side.

"I don't know." She held it up toward the bay window, trying to catch some of the dim lamplight outside the building. "Can you read this?"

Fred peered at it. It was plain, white, computer printer paper. Somebody had folded it a bunch of times and scrawled something on it—a brief note. *That handwriting!* He knew it from somewhere . . . yeah, it was definitely familiar. Very familiar. He strained his eyes.

Phil,

Great game, huh, prick? You might want to think about giving up this hobby of yours. Because when you promise somebody you're going to deliver 200 pizzas and then you don't, you leave a lot of people hungry. I got a family to feed, Phil. You know my family. When they get hungry, they get grouchy. Remember that New York City councilman? The Greek guy? He sidelined in the pizza business, too. Then he screwed up a bunch of deliveries. Now nobody can find him. He must have moved away.

You got until Saturday. Unless you want to lose something valuable.

The room spun. It hit Fred in a flash: He knew where he'd seen that handwriting before. It had graced his dartboard for the better part of a year. He gripped the desktop for support. His knees seemed to have vanished—along with the rest of his bones. He was nothing more than a quivering, gelatinous blob.

"What *is* this?" Sunday whispered.

"Salvatore," Fred gasped.

Sunday frowned at him. "Salvatore *who*? Salvatore Viverito?"

Fred nodded, swallowing. Acrid bile rose in his throat. "He must . . . he . . . ." Fred couldn't finish the thought.

"He what, Fred? He *what*?"

But Fred couldn't answer. Various memories and images swirled inside his head, in no particular order. Diane's face. Sal's jogging suit. The comment *"Nobody messes wit' da Viverito family."* An article he'd read last year about how real "made" guys were upset that *The Sopranos* portrayed their lifestyle so accurately. The tin of Old Hickory in Tony's book bag. A shovel. A bag of fertilizer. A pistol with a big fat silencer—

"What?" Sunday demanded. Her voice grew panicky. She tugged on his shirt. "What about Salvatore Viverito?"

"He's dating Diane," he heard himself whisper.

She shook her head. "I don't get it. Diane's your ex-girlfriend, right? What does that have to do with—"

"Look at that note, Sunday," Fred interrupted. His voice was hollow. "Salvatore's part of a 'family.' Do you get it now? Do you know what that means?"

Her eyes fell back to the note. She blinked several times. Suddenly she dropped it and jerked away, as if it were a hot potato. It fluttered down to the desk.

"Oh, my God," she breathed.

"My sentiments exactly," Fred mumbled. He shivered. He definitely should have worn a jacket. It was like a meat locker in here—*No, no*. Bad idea to think of meat lockers.

"He . . . ah . . . He . . . ah . . ." Sunday ran a hand through her hair.

"He thinks I got his kid brother expelled," Fred said. "He thinks I stole his girlfriend for a while. He's pissed at me, Sunday. Very pissed."

"Oh, man," Sunday said. She took a deep breath. "All right. All right. We can't wig out. We just have to stay calm."

Fred glanced out the window. Once again, the night's tranquillity stood in stark contrast to the ulcer that was surely festering inside him. *We can't wig out.* Why the hell not? When was it appropriate to wig out? Strange: Getting expelled didn't seem so bad anymore. Noah didn't know how lucky he was. Sure, his life would suck for a while—but, barring an unforeseen illness or accident, he'd *have* a life. He'd finish the year at public school, just like the majority of kids in America, and somewhere down the line, he'd inherit millions. Not bad. Not bad at all. Fred's own future wasn't looking as promising. Odds were good that *he* would finish the year at the bottom of the Connecticut River.

"Hey, Fred, check this out."

He turned to her. She'd pulled something else from the drawer: a manila folder.

"What are you doing?" he cried.

"What?" She opened it. A single sheet of paper was clipped inside.

"What do you mean, *what*?" Fred's voice rose. He couldn't help himself. "Sunday, we have to get out of here. Not just this building, this school. There might be a contract out on my life right now. Do you realize that?"

She glanced at him over the folder. "But you're safe here."

"Safe? Are you nuts?"

"Think about it, Fred," she said calmly. "Wessex is a boarding school. These are private grounds. So don't worry, okay? There's no way any mobster will come here to get you. It would be too risky. The campus is crawling with security."

"Security?" he yelled. "Are you kidding me? Do you think a hit man would be scared off by Planet Biff? Or Sparkles?"

"*Shh,*" Sunday whispered. Her eyes fell back to the folder. Then she handed it to Fred. "Just look at this for a second."

Fred scowled, but he stared down at the page.

<u>OPERATION</u> <u>TIME</u> <u>CAPSULE</u>

1998
Subject: GT
Asking price: $75,000.00

Breakdown
PO: $25,000.00
WE: $25,000.00
PB: $10,000.00
TR: $15,000.00
Status: *Complete*

1999
Subject: WC
Asking price: $100,000.00

Breakdown
PO: $35,000.00
WE: $35,000.00
PB: $10,000.00
JL: $20,000.00
Status: *Complete*

                    2000
               Subject: MR
Asking price: $125,000.00

               Breakdown
          PO: $50,000.00
          WE: $50,000.00
          PB: $10,000.00
          JH: $15,000.00
          Status: *Complete*

                    2001
               Subject: NP
Asking price: $200,000.00

               Breakdown
          PO: $100,000.00
          WE: $100,000.00
          PB1:   N/A
          PB2:   N/A
          Status: *Pending*

"What do you think this is?" Sunday asked.

Fred shook his head. His heart was beating too wildly for him to answer right away. "I think it's . . . something bad," he finally managed to whisper.

Sunday nodded, sidling up next to him. "What do you think those initials mean? I bet—"

The door crashed open.

It was Burwell.

Tonight's double-breasted suit was black. Or maybe navy blue. It was too dark to tell.

"You kids have really done it this time," he whispered. "I trailed you here from Ellis."

Fred just looked at him. Frankly, he was relieved. He was half-expecting Salvatore or one of his mob cronies to burst in here, wielding a machine gun. Seeing Burwell right now was like seeing an old friend. The fat oaf's surprise ambushes couldn't possibly faze Fred anymore. Not that they'd fazed him much in the past. No, unless Burwell was packing an Uzi himself, dealing with him would be an annoyance, at most. Like waiting in line at the DMV. How could Burwell threaten them? What could he do? Make another four-pronged bargain? Kick them out? Great! Hallelujah! Bring it on! Fred's only regret was that he hadn't broken Winnie's face. But there might still be time for that.

"Not so fast," Sunday stated defiantly. She waved the folder in the air.

Burwell stepped forward. "What do you have there?"

"Evidence that'll get you and Olsen and everybody else sent to prison," she said. "*You're* the one who's done it this time. You're cooked."

Fred cast her a sidelong glance. Unless she was a lot sharper than he'd previously suspected (and she was pretty damn sharp) there was no way she could have deduced that the gibberish on the paper was *evidence* against Burwell and Olsen—*Wait.* A delicious possibility occurred to him. Maybe she was calling Burwell's bluff. He grinned. Of course she was. Ha! Sunday Winthrop. She had some serious moxie, that girl. She was fast on her feet, a constant jack-in-the-box of surprises. Fred *never* would have thought of that. She was sharp, all right. Hypodermic-needle sharp.

"What do you mean, *evidence*?" Burwell spat. "Let me see that." He stomped forward and lunged across the desk, but Sunday whisked the folder just out of his reach.

"Uh-uh." She clucked her tongue. "Not yet. First you have to make some assurances."

Burwell glared at her. He straightened and smoothed his suit. "I have to make *you* insurances," he said. "You gotta be kidding me."

She raised her eyebrows. "Do you want to see this or not?"

"Give me the goddamn file, Winthorp."

"Winthrop," she corrected. "I'll give you the file as soon as you promise you'll keep this little visit among ourselves. Oh, and by the way?" She patted her peacoat pocket. "There's a Dictaphone in here. I use it to practice French. Sometimes it also comes in handy for taping conversations like these, in case I might have to divulge what we discuss to certain third parties. So it isn't wise to lie right now. You know what I'm saying?"

Burwell didn't answer. His eyes darted from the folder, to Fred, to Sunday, then back to the folder again.

"Your choice," Sunday said. "Maybe I should call my dad and ask him to cancel that meeting he's setting up with Joel Katzenberg—"

"Fine," Burwell snapped. "I promise."

"You promise what? Speak into the coat, please."

"To keep this little visit among ourselves," he grumbled through clenched teeth.

"Good." She handed the folder to him. "Now that was easy, wasn't it?"

Fred exchanged a quick smile with her. *That's my Sunday.* The Dictaphone BS was a stroke of genius. Pure genius.

Burwell stared at the page. He lifted it a little. Then a little more. He brought it closer and closer to his face . . . closer and closer, almost until it touched his nose. Then his hands started shaking. The manila made wobbly noises.

"Those bastards," he hissed.

Without another word, he dropped the file on the desk and stormed out of the office, slamming the door behind him.

Fred glanced at Sunday, dumbfounded.

"I wasn't expecting *that*," she said.

"I, uh . . . neither was I," he agreed. But after everything he'd experienced in the past few weeks, he knew there was no point in speculating about its significance, either. He turned to the grandfather clock. It was almost ten. "Do you think Burwell's going back to Ellis? Because if he is, I should probably be getting back, myself. I don't want to be late for check-in."

Sunday shrugged. "Better to be on the safe side," she said. She picked up the folder and tucked it into her peacoat.

"Right," Fred said, watching her. He could definitely feel that ulcer now. "The safe side."

Note Slipped Under Burwell's Apartment Door

Interoffice memorandum

To: PB
From: PO
Date: 10/17
Re: Sunday Winthrop

Paul, no need to apologize for communicating by paper. We all have to do what we can until the Internet server is repaired. And I apologize for the delay in my response. I've had my hands full, as you can well imagine. In any case, I appreciate your telling me about Sunday. I'm just relieved that one of us was here to monitor the campus during the game. I don't believe it's necessary to dismiss her, however. Nor is it necessary to dismiss Fred. They're just up to some childish fun. Every year, seniors sneak into my house to play pranks. It's tradition. While we certainly can't condone it, it's not worthy of drawing attention to it with such a severe punishment. As far as our operations go, we don't have anything to fear from them.

Our most pressing concern right now is Miss Burke. She's gotten out of hand. I need your help on this matter, Paul. You're the only one I can trust. Winslow Ellis isn't mature enough to handle this. I need you to do me a favor. I need you to take care of her. I'd suggest using the abandoned quarry. It's remote, secluded, and difficult to explore. Do we understand each other? I'm certain we do.

Letter from Travis Crowe to
Headmaster Olsen

Phil:

Steal an inch, steal a mile, right? Is that it? That was some stunt you pulled, tricking all of us into betting for the team this year. Was that your idea? Or was it your cannoli-eating partner's? Do you honestly think you can swindle me out of 20 grand? I don't know what you were thinking by having your boy Fred throw the game, but you just screwed yourself. That business with Walker was one thing. That was a cheap, miserable scam, but this is an insult. If there's one thing I hate in this world, it's being insulted by an idiot. So forget the gym. Forget the donations. All bets are off. I'm not afraid of your mobbed-up friends, either. Here's the deal: Unless you want me to bring you down for good, you're going to pay me that 20 thousand dollars and keep your mouth shut until Hobson graduates. Then you'll never hear from the Crowes again. If you're lucky.

                        —Travis

Part V
Things to Do on a Saturday Night at Boarding School

14

If Allison had to pick one school activity she could do without, it would most certainly be SNL, the biweekly Saturday night dance at Remsen Gym.

Nobody knew for certain why the dance had been nicknamed "SNL." It was just one of those labels that had somehow stuck. According to the most popular rumor, Bill Murray's niece had been a student here during the '80s, and he'd come to visit her once—and at the dance, he'd grabbed the microphone and shouted: "Live from New Farmington, it's Saturday Night!" It was just as reasonable an explanation as any other.

Attendance wasn't mandatory, of course. But unless you had serious problems, you were *there*—decked out in your finest, regardless of your social standing or clique. And Allison had never understood why. SNL seemed to foster a sick need in people to make utter fools of themselves. Her friends included. There were better ways to pass the time than mimicking a seizure to the accompaniment of techno. But Mackenzie and Sunday didn't agree. Almost every SNL found them out on the gym floor—leading a conga line, or doing the lambada with somebody like Carter Boyce, or clapping their hands and hooting when Hobson tried to break-dance.

Except for tonight.

No, apparently, on this particular Saturday night, they'd made other plans—without bothering to tell her, of course. She stood at the top of the bleachers, unconsciously grinding her teeth in time to the monotonous thud of yet another indistinguishable song. For maybe the tenth time in five minutes, she scanned each cluster of gyrating imbeciles for her two supposed best friends. *Not there . . . not there . . .* There was Carter Boyce. But he was dancing with a couple of slutty juniors: Alicia and Amanda. She didn't know their last names, and she didn't care to. They were the kinds of girls who bought cigarettes from Winnie. They were probably trying to lure Carter into a ménage-à-trois.

That was another thing she hated about SNL: the anything-goes, faux-rave atmosphere. It was no secret that some of these kids were on Ecstasy. (Alicia and Amanda among them, no doubt.) Yet the administration almost seemed to go out of its way to encourage loose behavior. Every week brought something new and outrageous—bigger speakers, faster strobe lights, video screens, a smoke machine. Tonight's special feature was a "drum circle"—a bunch of bongos carted over from the Music Lab, at the DJ's request. They were set up next to his DJ booth. Everybody took turns trying to bang along to the beat.

Allison would be lucky to make it out of here without a migraine.

She'd even complained about SNL to Olsen once, freshman year—after she'd caught a whiff of beer on Walker Crowe's breath. (She'd left his name out of the complaint, of course.) And what had Olsen said to her—condescendingly, she might add?

"For God's sake, a pot of small ale! Heh-heh-heh. We can't watch everybody all the time, Allison. All teenagers experiment."

Maybe that was true—although she had no idea what the "small ale" part meant. Maybe teenagers *did* need to experiment. Maybe that was why Hobson felt it necessary to try to spin on his head. Or worse, attempt The Worm. But he was nowhere to be found tonight, either—

"Hey, Al. What are you doing here all by your lonesome?"

She turned. Winnie was standing behind her, sipping from a plastic cup. He smiled. "Oh, wait," he said. "I've used that line before, haven't I?"

"Where is everybody?" she demanded.

"I don't know," he said. He lowered his eyes, then walked away.

"Wait! Winnie." She darted after him. "Are you all right? You look depressed."

He shrugged. "I guess I am a little depressed," he mumbled. "It's been kind of a stressful week. Things haven't really gone according to plan."

She frowned. "What things?"

"You know," he said. He took another sip. "Things."

"Oh, right." She placed her hands on her hips. "Things involving, say, a special committee? And a cell phone? And some guy named Sal?"

He smirked. "Something like that. Hey, can I ask you something, Al?"

"Sure," she said.

"Does Olsen ever piss you off?"

"Piss me off? What do you mean?"

"You know, does he ever say things that get on your nerves? Does he ever worry too much? Or try to come off as being holier-than-thou?"

She stared suspiciously at him. "What are you talking about, Winnie?"

He drained the rest of his soda, then crumpled

the cup and tossed it in the garbage. "Never mind," he muttered. "So. Do you wanna dance?"

"*Dance*?" She laughed. "With you? What are you, crazy?"

He lowered his eyes again.

"No, no, Winnie—I didn't mean it like that." She patted his arm. "I just meant . . . I mean, come on. You know me. When have you ever seen me dance at all? With anybody?"

"At Hobson's birthday party last year, you *tried* to dance," he said.

Allison's heart stirred. That was true. She'd tried to do the box step. But she couldn't reminisce about that—at least, not yet, anyway.

"Why don't you dance with Hadley Bryant?" she suggested.

Winnie made a sour face. "Hadley? No, thanks."

She sighed. "Well, I'm going to try to find Mackenzie and Sunday," she said. "Wanna come with me?"

He shook his head. "Nah. I'm gonna hang here."

"All right. I'll probably see you later on tonight."

The cold night air was a big relief. So was the silence. That stupid techno beat would probably ring through her head until she fell asleep. Par for the course, she supposed. She dug her hands into her pockets and hunched forward, hurrying down the gravel path toward Reed Hall. There was a chance Sunday and Mackenzie had just decided to stay in for the night. Maybe they just didn't want to deal with SNL. Everybody was still pretty freaked out about Noah's expulsion, after all.

Yeah . . . actually, until now, that hadn't even occurred to her. Of *course* they weren't at the dance. They were too sad about Noah.

She picked up her pace, feeling better. Personally—although she'd never, ever admit this to either one of them—she wasn't entirely displeased with the whole turn of events. As far as she was concerned, Noah should have been kicked out years ago. There was something wrong with him. That much was obvious. He needed help. Now maybe he could get it. This was really the best solution both for Noah and the school.

The only part that upset her was the fallout: the rumor mill that had started churning in the wake of his departure. *Nobody* deserved that kind of abuse, not even somebody like Noah. The poor boy was unbalanced. So he'd had a breakdown of some sort. But he certainly hadn't had sex with Miss Burke, or trashed his own room, or sabotaged the school's Internet service provider—as people were claiming. That was just talk. Mean-spirited, insecure talk . . .

She frowned.

Mackenzie's window was dark. All the Reed Hall

windows were dark. But maybe she and Sunday were in Sunday's room; her window was on the other side of the dorm.

Allison hurried up the stairs to the triple.

Then she paused.

They *were* in Mackenzie's room.

Or somebody was, anyway. She could hear whispering. The secret boy, maybe? *That* would be juicy. She tiptoed over to the door and pressed her ear against it.

". . . what I'm trying to tell you, sweetie."

Mackenzie. That was her, all right. Allison grinned. Sweetie, eh? There *had* to be a boy in there. Well, unless Mackenzie and Sunday had decided to do some "experimenting." *Eww.* Now that she thought about it, she wouldn't put it past them—not after what she'd seen at Olsen's house, the night of the Student Council Dinner.

"I was checking into your most recent past life," Mackenzie continued. "And you know what? I'm almost positive you're the reincarnation of Pig Pen. He was this rock star who went out with Janis when they lived in San Francisco. Isn't that insane? It's, like, we've already *been* together, in the past."

"Pig Pen? No way! I can't be somebody named *Pig Pen*! That's ill, yo!"

Allison stopped grinning.

"Yo, I think I was Malcolm X. For real—"

"Hobson!" Allison shouted. White-hot rage flashed through her. It was like a bolt of electricity, a thousand muscle spasms at once. She grabbed the doorknob. It was locked. She gave it a savage tug, eyes blazing. "Open up!"

"Oh, my God," Mackenzie gasped. "Allison, is that you?"

"Of course it's me, dammit! What are you doing in there? Why are the lights off?"

Nobody answered. Allison pounded on the door.

"Just . . . okay, just give me a second, Al, all right?" Mackenzie stammered. "I'm really, really . . . oh, boy. This doesn't look good. Wait! Hobson! What are you—"

The door flew open.

Hobson stood there, decked out in a jeans-and-sweatshirt combination large enough to fit about eight guys at once. His hair was in disarray.

"I'm sorry, Al," he said. "We shoulda told you."

"Told me what?" Unfortunately, the words were garbled; Allison's jaw had seized up. The question sounded more like, *Trrd mrr wrrt.*

"Pardon?" Hobson said.

"Never mind." *Nrrr Mrrr.* She peered into the shadows. Mackenzie was sitting on the Sven Larsen futon that Allison had picked out for her. That *Allison* had picked out for *her.* As a suitemate. A sister. The sheets were rumpled. Well. Not a lot of gray area there. No, her best friend (or one of them, anyway) was making out with her boyfriend. Or maybe they were just kissing. Third base. Holding hands. It didn't really matter. Whatever the degree of intimacy, they had succeeded in their mission: They had chopped Allison's heart out with an ax and discarded the pieces in a trash compactor.

Allison didn't get it. *Hobson* was the secret boy? How was that possible? This was like some bad movie plot. Or worse. It was so ridiculous and hackneyed and over-the-top that it couldn't be real. But it was. And that meant she had to put as much distance between herself and the situation as possible. Now. She turned and walked out of the suite.

"Allison!" Mackenzie called. "Wait!"

Good line, Mackenzie. She stomped down the stairs. That was almost as original as the act of betrayal itself. What next? *"I'm sorry?"*

"I'm sorry!" Mackenzie shouted.

Allison slammed the front door and took off down the path. She knew exactly where she was headed, too. Yes, sir. Mackenzie had shed her phony mask to reveal the foul seductress within. Sunday had, as well. And Hobson had shed *his* mask to reveal his inner Judas. Now it was her turn. She would do something selfish and wicked and unexpected. *With* somebody selfish and wicked and unexpected. Of course! She would show all of them. Because she didn't need them anymore. She didn't need anybody but *him*: the one person who might possibly understand her, the one person who didn't try to conceal his deceit. . . .

"Winnie!" she panted.

He was walking toward her down the path, hands in his pockets, a vision in khakis.

"Hey," he called to her. "Good thing I ran into you. The dance was lame. I changed my mind. I decided to come find you guys—"

"Winnie, do you find me attractive?" she demanded. She planted herself in front of him.

He stared at her. "Excuse me?"

"Do you find me attractive?"

"Well . . . um, yeah," he said. He laughed, bewildered. "I mean, everybody does. You look just like Nicole—"

"Don't say it," she breathed. She gave him a quick once-over. He *wasn't* bad looking. No. He was big and solid and real. There was no danger that he'd ever spin on his head or buy a fourteen-thousand-dollar pair of turntables. He was comfortable with who and what he was: an AB, the sole heir to the Ellis fortune. He just needed a girlfriend. That was all.

"Uh . . . what's this all about?" he asked.

She grabbed his hand and veered off the path,

leading him toward the woods. "Nothing. I'm glad you find me attractive. That's all. I find you attractive, too."

"Uh . . . that's great, Allison. Thanks. But where are we going right now?"

"To the Waldorf," she said.

"The Waldorf. Okay. What are we gonna do there?"

"We're going to forget about things for a while. How does that sound?"

His fingers intertwined with her own. "Actually, that sounds just about perfect—"

"Oh, but Winnie?" She stopped and turned to him for a second.

"Yeah?"

"Second base is my limit."

He grinned. "Mine, too."

"Good," she said. "It's wise to settle these things in advance."

"I couldn't agree more," Winnie said.

Allison smiled at him. People always underestimated the value of simple companionship. Why was that?

Note Pinned to Allison's Door

Dear Al,

What can I possibly say? I know you must hate me. I would hate me. I _do_ hate me. I mean, not really, but I hate myself for hurting you and for not being honest with you sooner. I guess I just wasn't being honest with myself.

See, Allison, Hobson and I

Let me start over. I don't know how to say this, exactly. I'm pretty lousy with words! But you already know that. I guess that's kind of my point. We've been friends for such a long, long time. We both expect things to work out in certain ways. You had your heart set on Hobson for so many years. You thought that he was your soul mate. And because of that, I thought he was, too.

I mean, it's pretty amazing when you think about it. I ignored all this important stuff, like the fact that he's a Taurus and you're a Leo. And then there are your rising signs and inner planets. You guys just aren't a great match, Allison. And I know that's probably the last thing you want to hear right now. But I have to tell you the truth, because I didn't want to believe it, either. I wanted you guys to be together so badly. Really. That's how I started fooling around with Hobson in the first place.

Okay, I know that makes no sense, but I have to see you face-to-face to try to explain it all. You're one of my best friends, Al. I never, ever want to lose that.

When I'm mad at somebody, I think about fun things we did together, so that I won't let the mad energy affect my inner balance. It's like, when Buster has an accident and poops all over my bedroom, I don't get mad. I think about playing Frisbee with him in the backyard. I guess that's what I'm saying. If you can find it within yourself, think of me like Buster. Think of all the times we played Frisbee.

xoxoxoxo—
Mack

P.S. I'm really sorry. Hobson is, too.

Letter from Charles Percy to Phillip Olsen

Mr. Charles Percy
32 Deer Run Lane
Sherman, CT 06578

The Honorable Headmaster Phillip Olsen
The Wessex Academy
41 South Chapel Street
New Farmington, Connecticut 06744

October 19

Dear Phillip,

Thank you for your letter. I appreciate your candor.

You mentioned that you were doubtful an arrangement could be made. I'm a businessman, so I know what that means. You already have a figure in mind. Why don't you name it, and then we can put this foolishness behind us. Forgive me for being so blunt, but I have very little spare time, and I can't spend it bargaining to keep my son in school. We've known each other a long time. They don't call me "Big Bucks" Chuck for nothing.

That was an attempt at levity.

While we're on the subject, when will Noah be returned to us? Susan and I are getting a little concerned. It's been two days, and we still haven't heard a word from him. Paul Burwell informed me that his room was cleaned out Monday. Is he being held on campus for some reason?

I trust I will hear from both you and Noah shortly.

Yours,
Charles Percy

15

Sunday hadn't journeyed to the old, abandoned quarry by Highway 91 since sophomore year. And that was precisely why she'd dragged Fred out here tonight. Nobody would consider looking for them in this wretched place, because the only students who ever bothered with the arduous forty-five-minute bike ride were troublemakers with lots to hide: chronic drug users, pyromaniacs, alcoholics . . .

Or Fred and me.

Right. Whoops. Maybe people *would* come looking for them. But at least the quarry was safer than campus. For the time being . . . unless, of course, Burwell had tailed them again, which was a distinct possibility. *Ugh.* They were alone for now; that was the important thing. Even the pyromaniacs had decided to stick around for

SNL. There was going to be a "drum circle" tonight. Apparently, this was cause for excitement.

Sunday envied people who found that exciting. She truly did.

The cliff overlooking the vast, man-made crater was as dark and deserted as ever—littered with the same old garbage: fast-food wrappers, empty liquor bottles, cigarette butts. Moonlight glistened on the stagnant pond far below. (The fact that people actually jumped into that water was beyond her. The drop was a hundred feet, at least. A state of altered consciousness was clearly required.) It was eerie; everything was just as she remembered it. Exactly. This place was frozen in time. Like that stairwell Hobson had found in McNeil House last year. Nobody had even bothered adding any new graffiti since her last visit. The most recent message, spray-painted in black on the opposite wall, was still BURY THE MEATSTICK, CLASS OF '96!

"Hey, I meant to ask you something," Fred said. He leaned his bike against a tree. "You don't still have that folder, do you? You put it back in Olsen's desk, right?"

She smiled faintly. "Of course. First thing in the morning, before classes," she said. "The only reason I took it was to copy everything down." She sat in the clearing that sloped down toward the cliff's edge, then fished a scrap of paper from her peacoat pocket. She was actually pretty proud of herself for having handled

Burwell so well that night. No, make that *very* proud. Performing under pressure had never been her forte.

"Is that the copy?" Fred asked, sitting beside her.

Sunday nodded. "Yeah." She squinted at the paper in the moonlight. *Operation Time Capsule.* The name gave her the willies—not only because it was so childish and corny, but also because Olsen always maintained that he never looked through the time capsule submissions. *"That would compromise the integrity of the whole exercise,"* he'd told her on the first day of classes. *"We want students to feel free to write whatever they want, to say whatever they feel. That way the students of the future will get a real, objective, unbiased look at what's going on here today. . . ."*

Yeah, right. *He* was getting an objective, unbiased look at what was going on. That was how he chose his victims. According to Sunday's theory, anyway. But it was a damn good theory, if she said so herself. She felt a little like the FBI woman from *The Silence of the Lambs* movies. She'd glimpsed the inner workings of a narcissistic psychopath and dissected them. She wouldn't be surprised if Olsen ate people, as well—like Hannibal Lecter.

"What do you think those initials mean?" Fred asked.

"I think PO stands for Phillip Olsen," she said. "WE stands for Winslow Ellis. PB and PB-one both stand for Paul Burwell. I don't know about these others. Although I'm guessing NP stands for Noah Percy, and PB-two stands for Patricia Burke. See, I bet Noah wrote something really ridiculous in his time capsule submission, like, 'I want to have sex with a teacher.' Then Olsen set it up. He used that videotape to bribe him. And then something went wrong, so Olsen expelled him."

Fred nodded. "That's what Noah meant by 'two hundred grand' in the note," he whispered. He sounded as if he were talking to himself. "That was the bribe."

"The note? What note?"

"The note Noah left me," Fred mumbled. He leaned close to her, staring down at the crumpled page. "I bet that's why Burwell was so pissed that night," he breathed. "That's why he stormed out of the office. Olsen and Winnie have been taking most of the money. Look at those numbers. He's been getting less and less. This year, he isn't even getting any money at *all*. Neither is Miss Burke. N-slash-A." He glanced up at her. "What do you think that means?"

"I think it means 'not applicable,'" she said.

Fred frowned. "Really? But that—"

She started kissing him.

She had no idea why. It was an instantaneous reaction to some hidden force; all of a sudden, the urge to kiss him was too powerful to resist. Maybe it had something to do with how cute he looked in the moonlight, or how his eyes glittered like two perfect pebbles, or how the recent overdose of terror had turned her brain to gruel. Whatever. She couldn't control herself. She ran her hands through his hair, pulling him closer—

"Wait," Fred murmured. He leaned away from her. "I'm sorry. I just . . . I just have to tell you something, okay?"

"What? Is something wrong?"

He shook his head. "No. I mean, yes. Not with *you*, though. Not with what we're doing. It's just . . ." He lowered his eyes for a second, then looked at her again. "Here's the thing. Noah's totally in love with you, Sunday. He always has been. I just feel guilty, I guess. That's all. You know, especially *now*."

Sunday nodded. Her hands fell away from Fred's shoulders. She'd always known that Noah was in love with her, of course; everybody had. But that "love" wasn't anything real. It was a harmless crush, something abstract, not to be taken seriously. Or so she'd categorized it. And deep down, that was how she'd always categorized Noah himself: He wasn't to be taken seriously. Which might explain why she hadn't allowed herself to think too hard about his expulsion. She swallowed. Guilt was beginning to wrap its icy tentacles around her. She wanted to cry. *And* keep kissing Fred—if that made any sense.

"I'm sorry," Fred whispered. "I shouldn't have said anything."

"No, no . . . I'm glad you did." Her voice was thick. She smiled sadly. "Not many . . . not many guys are like you, Fred. You know that? You're . . ." She hesitated.

A car was approaching. It was coming at them pretty fast, judging by the whine of the engine. Maybe somebody *had* trailed them here. She turned toward the sound, then glanced at Fred. His eyes were like saucers. He grabbed her hand and dashed out of the clearing on the cliff's edge into some nearby woods.

No . . . it was two cars. It seemed like they were drag racing—straight toward the quarry. Could they be townies, maybe?

Headlights swept across the cliff side, skirting the leaves and branches in front of them. Sunday held her breath and ducked behind a tree trunk. She shut her eyes, clinging to one of Fred's pant legs as if it were a life preserver.

The cars screeched to a halt, not ten yards away.

The lights and engines went dead.

Please be townies, please be—

A door opened. Then another. Then a third. There were footsteps.

"What the hell do you think you're doing?" a voice barked.

Oh, my God. It *was* Burwell.

"Shut up," somebody else snapped.

Fred jerked. His leg trembled. Sunday opened her eyes. That voice was familiar. Fred crouched beside her. "Salvatore," he whispered.

Sunday started hyperventilating.

"Who are *you*?" a woman asked.

Fred glanced at Sunday. Yes, she knew that voice, too. "Miss Burke," she mouthed. Fred nodded. He turned back toward the clearing. But she couldn't look. It was too terrifying. She closed her eyes again. Her breath came in rapid gasps.

"Sal, what the hell are you doing?" Burwell shouted. "Put that thing away—"

"I said, shut up," Salvatore interrupted. "Get in the car. Now. Move it!"

"Bu-but," Miss Burke started stammering. "I didn't—"

"Lady, if you don't shut up, I'm just gonna shoot you right now. Okay?"

No, no, no. Had Sunday heard that correctly? Had he said—yes, he had. *Shoot you right now.* She was absolutely certain that she would have a heart attack. Her pulse was faster than it had ever been, yet there was no meter or rhythm; it was firing like a pinball machine gone berserk. She only prayed that she wouldn't utter any last dying gasps when she finally succumbed. If she went quickly, Fred might still have a chance of escaping.

Two doors slammed shut.

What happened next was uncertain. . . . There were some muffled protests, a lot of vicious thumping . . . then silence. Sunday's body tensed. Fred stood up straight. She knew she couldn't keep hiding like an ostrich with her head in the sand. She *had* to see what was going on. *Do it!* She turned and opened her eyes.

Tree limbs obscured the view, but she was still able to catch a glimpse of a redheaded figure in a jogging suit, hunched over the driver's side of Burwell's beat-up old Chevy. *Salvatore.* He'd put on a little weight since he'd graduated. The old freshman fifteen, she supposed. (If he'd even attended college.) He fiddled with something inside the car, then slammed the door and dashed away—back to his own car, a bright red Camaro.

Burwell's Chevy started rolling down the slope toward the cliff.

Sunday watched it pick up speed.

She knew in her heart that a very, very bad sequence of events was unfolding—leading toward only one inevitable conclusion. But she was powerless to do anything but stare. The car gained momentum, bouncing slightly. Then it vanished over the edge of the cliff.

Just like that. Without a sound.

Several seconds later, there was a deep, distant splash. It was surprisingly quiet.

The Camaro's headlights lit up. Tires squealed. Dust flew as the car shot backward, then spun around—screaming off into the night.

After a minute or so, the quarry was still again.

"What just happened?" Sunday asked.

She hoped that if she asked the question, she'd

miraculously wake up in bed—like when Dorothy tapped her ruby slippers in *The Wizard of Oz*. Not the dorm bed, either. Her *real* bed. The four-poster bed. In Greenwich. Surrounded by throw pillows and old stuffed animals. And this would all prove to be some long, vivid, awful nightmare.

Unfortunately, it didn't seem to be working.

"We just witnessed a murder," Fred said.

Sunday nodded. She was very close to vomiting up the veal marsala she'd eaten for dinner. "That's what I thought," she said.

"We just saw Salvatore Viverito kill Mr. Burwell and Miss Burke," he added.

"Yeah." She blinked a few times. "Right."

Neither of them spoke for a moment.

"So," Fred finally said. "Now do you believe that the Mafia can get to people at boarding school?" His voice was toneless.

"Bu-bu-but they weren't on school grounds," Sunday stammered. She didn't even know what she was trying to say. "I mean, neither are we."

"You're right," Fred said. "And we're never going back to school grounds again."

She looked at him. "We aren't?"

"No. We're out of here. Out of Wessex. For good."